THE SEAL'S SECOND CHANCE BABY

BY
LAURA MARIE ALTOM

MILLS &
BOON

First Published in Great Britain 2016
By Mills & Boon, an imprint of HarperCollins*Publishers*
1 London Bridge Street, London, SE1 9GF

© 2016 Laura Marie Altom

ISBN: 978-0-263-91995-0

23-0616

Our policy is to use papers that are natural, renewable and recyclable products and made from wood grown in sustainable forests. The logging and manufacturing processes conform to the legal environmental regulations of the country of origin.

Printed and bound in Spain
by CPI, Barcelona

Laura Marie Altom is a bestselling and award-winning author who has penned nearly fifty books. After college (Go, Hogs!), Laura Marie did a brief stint as an interior designer before becoming a stay-at-home mum to boy-girl twins and a bonus son. Always an avid romance reader, she knew it was time to try her hand at writing when she found herself replotting the afternoon soaps.

When not immersed in her next story, Laura plays video games, tackles Mount Laundry and, of course, reads romance!

Laura loves hearing from readers at either PO Box 2074, Tulsa, OK 74101, USA or by email, balipalm@aol.com.

Check out www.lauramariealtom.com to win fun stuff!

This story is dedicated to my precious family:
Terry, Not-So-Little-Anymore Terry, Hannah
& her sweet Steven, Russell, Mom & Dad,
and my adopted sisters—Margaret & Amy.
You all make my life worth living. xoxo

Chapter One

Effie Washington stopped humming to hold her hand to her forehead, shading her eyes from the brutal August sun. Was she seeing a mirage? Was that a mule deer or man on horseback, slumped in his saddle?

From her vantage atop the roof of her grandmother's run-down adobe ranch house, she narrowed her gaze. In southeast Colorado, judging distance could be tricky. On a clear day, she had the front range to her west, but with miles upon miles of rolling grassland and the vast wide-open sky, the object she thought might be a few hundred yards in the distance could turn out to be a mile away.

"Colt! Remington!" she called to her six-year-old identical-twin boys. They were supposed to be on ladder guard duty—a fancy way of ensuring they didn't run off by making them believe they were charged with a highly important job.

"Yeah, Mom?" As usual, they answered in tandem.

"Did you ever put your boots back on after I caught you messing with the hose?"

"Uh-uh," Remington said.

"I will now!" Colt darted around the side of the house. Remington followed.

A few minutes of silence alerted Effie to the chance that her angels were up to no good.

"Cool! A scorpion!"

She peered over the roof to find both boys beneath the yard's sole tree—a century-old cottonwood—engrossed in poking a stick at the potentially harmful creature.

"Leave it alone!" Effie closed her eyes and sighed. Those two would be the death of her. At least once she finally finished her nursing degree, she'd know how to tend to most of their health emergencies. Abandoning the much-needed roof-patching project, she hurried down the ladder to disperse her boys, who not only hadn't left the scorpion alone, but had scooped it into a tin can they'd snatched from the trash barrel.

"But it's awesome!" Colt jabbed a weed at it to watch it rear up and strike.

"Quit!" Remington shouted. "He's gonna sting my eyeballs!"

"Give me that." Effie took the can, carrying it far from the house to fling the offensive creature over the back fence.

"Aw, why'd you have to go and do that?" Colt pouted. "We was gonna take it to school."

"*We were going* to take it—and since school doesn't start for another week—no, no and no."

"You're mean!" Colt kicked a dirt clump near the toe of his boot.

"But I love you." *Sometimes*, Effie silently added with secret smile. Motherhood had never been easy—her twins had been a challenge from day one. "How about you get in the house and see if Grandma needs help with Cassidy?"

Colt scrunched his face. "We don't wanna go inside. Grandma's always watchin' her stupid *soap boperas*, and Cass is boring."

"Go!" Effie pointed toward the back door. "If Grandma doesn't need help, clean your room."

With the twins grumbling and moping their way into the house, Effie scanned the horizon for the odd sight that had started all of this. Once Colt had his boots back on, she'd intended to send the boys off to scout the situation, but she could now plainly see a chestnut with its rider hunched in the saddle a good hundred yards north of the house.

The four-wheeler was busted, and it would take longer to saddle her trusty paint, Lulu, than it would to walk, so Effie tugged the brim of her straw cowboy hat lower to shade against the sun, then trudged through thick weeds and grasses, dotted with occasional cactus and yucca. They'd had surprisingly good rain throughout the summer, which meant her herd of thirty Angus was fat and happy.

They sold them off as needed for extra income.

The closer she came to the man, the more obvious it became that he was in trouble, Effie started to run.

"Hello? Can you hear me?" By the time she reached him and his horse, she was out of breath and sweat drenched. The sun's heat pressed her shoulders like malevolent hands.

The stranger was unconscious.

"Sir?" She shook him. Looked as though he might have tried using a rope to lash himself into the saddle, but it now hung loose. If his boot heels hadn't been stuck in the stirrups, he'd have fallen off. *Is he dehydrated?*

No. A nearly full water bottle hung from the saddle's horn.

His horse neighed, its eyes wide with panic.

"It's all right, boy." Knowing she needed to get this

man to a hospital, Effie took the horse by the reins, guiding him toward the house as fast as she could manage.

She didn't slow until she reached the yard's gate, and even then, she hollered, "Colt! Remington! Mabel!" Please, God, let them hear her through the open window screens.

All three came running. Her grandmother carried six-month-old Cass on her hip.

"Whoa!" the twins cried, racing to her.

"What happened to him?" Colt asked.

"Don't know." Effie led the man's horse into the only slightly cooler shade alongside the barn. "I need to call 911." Never had she wished more for the cell phone she'd left back at the house.

"Look at his hand." Remington pointed. "It's all puffy."

Effie paused a moment to look. The man's fingers had swollen to the point that his wedding ring would need to be cut off. Twin puncture wounds oozed a nasty mix of clear fluid and blood. She'd seen similar marks on a horse, and then only because she'd witnessed the rattlesnake strike.

She took off running toward the house.

"What's wrong with him, Mom?" Colt called after her.

"Snakebite," she heard Mabel say.

No doubt from the heat and excitement, just as Effie reached the front porch, Cassidy began to cry.

MARSH LANGTREE DRIFTED in and out of a strange new world.

His son, Tucker, was still alive, but older—and somehow there were two of him. A baby wouldn't stop crying. And then there was an angel—petite and blonde with eyes the same deep blue-green as the Indian Ocean.

Let's get that ring off and start an IV.

His eyes wouldn't stay open.

Mom, is he dead?

Maybe I am?

The angel knelt alongside him, stroking his hair. *You'll be all right. They're taking you to the hospital.*

Hospital? Marsh thought he'd died. That was the only way he'd ever see his son again.

A man approached with a tool and then there was pressure on his left hand. *Ma'am, would you mind holding his ring? He'll probably want to have it repaired when he comes out of this.*

Why were they taking his wedding ring?

Before he could further process the question, his eyes drifted closed and refused to open again.

"WE'LL BE TAKING him to Arkansas Valley Regional in La Junta," the older of the two paramedics said to Effie after they'd settled the man in the back of the ambulance. He handed her the stranger's wallet. She felt foolish for not having looked for it sooner. "Since he's gotta be from around here, would you please contact his family? This kind of news comes better from friends."

"Sure," she said automatically, hoping her grandmother might know the man's next of kin. "Is he going to be okay?"

"He'll live, but it's too soon to tell how much lasting damage there might be to his hand."

While the twins chased the ambulance down the dirt drive, Mabel approached with Cassidy still on her hip. "Sure didn't see any of this coming. Some bit of excitement, huh?"

"Yep." Excitement was one way of putting it. Effie's pulse still hadn't slowed.

Her grandmother wrangled the boys back into the house to help fix lunch. "You coming?"

"I will in a sec." Effie gravitated toward the barn. "Let me take care of the stranger's horse."

Effie led the chestnut into the cathedral-like barn, setting the wallet on top of a hay bale. The structure's ancient wood creaked in the light breeze. She never tired of the smells of hay and worn leather tack and a trace of manure.

Mabel had inherited the ranch from her third husband, Dwayne, a few years earlier. They'd celebrated their thirtieth anniversary before he died from cancer. He'd been a kind, loving man—far better than Effie's no-account grandfather, who'd gone to jail for cattle rustling a year after their vows.

Poor Mabel had then married his brother, but that marriage hadn't turned out much better. He'd been a moonshiner who'd gone and gotten himself shot and died a week later from his wound.

After leading the horse to a stall, Effie removed his saddle and set it atop a rack. She then brushed the creature, calming him with each stroke.

The adrenaline rush of finding the unconscious man had reminded her all too much of the first time she'd seen her own ex-husband, Moody, bucked from the back of a bull. He'd lain on the rodeo arena's soft dirt for a good five minutes before paramedics helped him come around. She'd been six months pregnant with the twins and feared going into early labor from the terror of finding her reckless husband paralyzed or dead.

That night marked the beginning of the end of their marriage—not because he'd been seriously injured, but because he hadn't. Instead of being relieved to the point that he gave up his PBR dreams to settle down with a nice, safe nine-to-five job, he'd doubled the amount of bull-riding competitions he entered. She'd prayed that once the boys were born he'd realize it was time to call it quits, but he refused.

She'd fooled herself into thinking love would be enough to sustain her through life on the road with newborns and then toddlers, but when the twins turned five and were eager to start school, she'd put her foot down, demanding Moody stop for the sake of their family.

He'd again refused, leaving her with no choice but to go on without him in the hopes that he'd soon miss her and the boys badly enough to realize he needed them more than adrenaline.

Her parents had offered to take her and the boys in, but they led such active lives back in Oklahoma City, where she'd grown up, that she couldn't imagine how she and the boys would fit in.

When Effie's widowed grandmother, Mabel, suggested it would be a godsend for Effie to move in and help, she'd jumped at the offer. Not for one second did she believe her high-octane, square-dance-a-holic grandma actually needed her, but she was beyond grateful for the safe place for her little family to land.

Once the twins started school, Moody visited whenever he had the chance, but those times dwindled to the point that if she hadn't been so determined to stand by her marriage vows, she might have considered asking for a divorce. Cassidy had been conceived the last time Effie had been with Moody. She'd been two months pregnant when he'd served her with divorce papers.

Wasn't something Effie liked thinking about, but far from missing their little family, he'd eventually swapped them for a hot-to-trot raven-haired barrel racer whose daddy had more money than God and the tricked-out trucks and matching horse trailers to prove it.

"Mom! Gramma says hurry up and come eat!"

Startled by Colt's interruption of the barn's peace and her chaotic thoughts, Effie dropped the horse brush to wipe tears she hadn't realized had been falling. "Coming!"

She knelt to retrieve the brush, then rose to smooth the chestnut's mane. "Guess you're probably ready for lunch, too, huh?"

The horse snorted.

"I'll take that as a yes." She filled his water trough and gave him plenty of hay and a scoop of grain.

Her mare, Lulu, was out to pasture, grazing.

"Mom! Come on!"

"Almost done," she said on her way out of the mystery horse's stall.

"What took you so long?" Colt met her at the barn's open door.

"The hurt man's horse was overheated. He needed brushing."

"Oh. How come your eyes are all red and puffy?"

"They are?" She swiped them again. "Must be the heat. What did Grandma make for lunch?"

He wrinkled his nose. "Grilled cheese sandwiches and tomato soup."

"Sounds good. I thought you loved her grilled cheese sandwiches?"

"Yeah, but when we were at Scotty's house on Sunday after church, his dad cooked steaks for lunch and then we went swimming and stuff. Why can't we ever do that here? And how come Dad doesn't want to see me anymore?"

Effie pressed her lips tight.

Where did she begin with telling her precious son that Daddy knocked up his girlfriend while he'd still been married to Mommy and now he had no interest in anyone but his new family? Then there was the not-so-little matter of child support checks that never seemed to come. Effie had dedicated her entire life to Moody. She'd even dropped out of nursing school one semester shy of graduating—stupid. But that was what love did to a girl. And she had loved that no-good cowboy with every breath of her being.

"Mom? Why can't we have steak? And a pool with a slide? And a house that's so cold inside that even in the summer Scotty's mom wears a big fur coat that looks like a fox."

Because your father is a low-down, two-timing snake who— No. She would never make the boys think their dad was anything less than the hero they believed him to be.

"Mom? I want a pool!" Colt gave up walking toward the house to hop.

"I'd like one, too." She caught up with him and planted her hand atop his head in an attempt to calm him. "Along with a giant bathtub and air-conditioning so cold I need a coat in the middle of summer, but we have something way better than all that."

"Like what?" The way Colt's chin touched his chest, he didn't look convinced.

"Love." She smoothed his hair. "Lots and lots of love."

"Yuck! That's gross!" He ran toward the house. "I want steak and a pool!"

Effie sighed.

Mabel leaned out the screen door. "Eff, hon, do you have that poor stranger's wallet?"

"I forgot it in the barn."

"Could you please get it?" Mabel asked. "I want to call his wife. She's no doubt beside herself with worry."

"Agreed." To her son, Effie said, "Colt, get in the house, and don't forget to thank Grandma for cooking."

"I don't want a stupid sandwich! I want steak!" Instead of joining his brother and sister inside as he'd been told, Colt darted around the back of the house.

"The boy needs a firm hand," Mabel noted.

"I know." *He needs his father.*

"Let him sulk for a bit. Might do him good." She glanced over her shoulder. "I see him through the bedroom window. He's sitting on the swing. Go ahead and grab the wallet, then get in here and eat before your soup gets cold."

"Yes, ma'am." In this heat, Effie doubted anything could get cold, but after swallowing the all-too-familiar knot at the back of her throat, she marched back to the barn.

At the moment, that poor stranger needed her help far more than her smart-mouthed son.

MARSH DRIFTED IN and out of consciousness.

We tried intubating on the way, but he was too combative. He's bleeding from the site, so we had to restrain him to keep him from pulling tubes out.

Light. So much light. He squinted against the fluorescent track's glare. Where was his boy? His wife? The angel who'd found him?

How much Crotalidae was given?

He got the initial six, and we're hanging another six right now.

"Sir? Could you tell us what kind of snake bit you?" Were they talking to him?

"Sir? Were you bitten by a rattlesnake?"

Marsh tried nodding but couldn't be sure if he'd even moved.

"Sir, judging by the severity of your symptoms, we need to double-check you weren't bitten by something more exotic. Are you sure it was a rattler?"

"Y-yes," Marsh managed. After having to put down one of his grandfather's best horses when it broke its leg in a prairie dog hole, Marsh had been out on the range, filling as many of the damned things as he could, when the snake lunged without warning. It clamped onto the webby flesh between his thumb and forefinger for an eternity before Marsh shook him free. He'd done his best to stay calm, drunk as much water as he could, then climbed into his chestnut's saddle, strapping himself in before aiming the horse for home.

Sounds definitive to me. Look at the poor guy. He's twitching all over. See the fasciculations? How his muscles look like worms under his skin. It's bad. One of the worst snakebites I've seen in a while.

Chapter Two

"Marsh Langtree…" Mabel held up the stranger's ID to check it with her reading glasses. "Why does that name sound familiar?"

"Is he a neighbor?" They'd finished lunch, and while Mabel fed Cassidy her baby food pears, Effie cleared the kitchen table. "I mean, think about it. I found him on horseback, so he couldn't have come from too far away."

"Hmm…" Mabel wiped drool from the baby's chin.

Cassidy grinned and blew a raspberry.

Effie's daughter had her blue eyes, but the twins had Moody's soulful brown gaze. Every time she looked at her boys, Effie could be bitter, but she was only thankful that her brief marriage had created such blessings.

"Seems to me—" Mabel fed Cassidy another bite "—Wallace Stokes has family out east."

"Who's Wallace?"

"Let's just say he's a neighbor and leave it at that."

"Why haven't you mentioned him before? You had to have known him, right?"

"Girl, leave it alone."

"I'm intrigued." Effie fitted the stopper in the sink, turned on hot water, then added a squirt of dish soap. "This sounds like a good story."

"Ha! He's got a fresh mouth."

"This just keeps getting better..." Effie didn't try hiding her grin. Mabel might be a great-grandma three times over, but that didn't stop her from flirting up a storm every Saturday night she went square dancing. "What did he do?"

"Poor Dwayne had barely been in his grave a year when Wallace showed up at the Grange Hall for dancing and told me I was shakin' my behind like a wet dog."

Effie tried not to laugh—really, she did—but Mabel's pinched scowl was too funny.

"How's that funny? The man's a scoundrel."

"Grandma, even you have to admit that when you've had a few beers—"

"I don't imbibe in spirits, and shame on you for inferring I do. I might have had cider, but that's all."

"If you say so." Effie winked.

"Girl, you'd better be glad you're too big for a spanking, or else."

"Sorry, Grandma. But do you have Wallace's phone number? If so, I'll give him a call to save you the trouble."

"Why would I have the old coot's number?"

"We could try calling information or looking it up online."

"Girl, I've got no patience for your fancy detective work. Go see him in person. It's that rock house a fair piece down the road with the leaning barn. Not only is the man foulmouthed, but lazy."

"I've never heard you say a bad word about anyone. Is this Wallace character really so bad?"

As if on cue, Cassidy spit out her last bite of pears.

"See?" Mabel said. "If even hearing about the man left a sour taste in this sweet baby's mouth, then you know what I say is true."

THIRTY MINUTES LATER, Effie had finished cleaning the lunch dishes, gotten the sulking twins started on their afternoon chores and allowed her grandmother to coerce her into visiting this supposedly wretched Wallace who might or might not have kin named Marsh Langtree.

She now stood on the man's front porch, wishing for even a hint of a breeze to cut the oppressive heat.

At least his yard sported three cottonwoods. She welcomed the shade.

Effie had just raised her hand to knock on the peeling red front door when it opened. Startled, she jumped back, pressing her hand over her pounding heart. "You scared me."

"Good. I don't need religion or a new vacuum, so you'd best be on your way."

"No, sir. I'm Effie Washington—your neighbor from down the road. My grandma says we share a property line with you, and—"

"Mabel's your grandmother?"

"Yessir…" Effie held her breath. If he harbored half as many hard feelings toward Mabel as she did toward him, this visit might turn even more unpleasant.

"Well, why didn't you say so? Come on in." He stepped back to hold open the door.

She entered, and nearly purred with pleasure from a humming window-mounted air conditioner's chill. "Wow, does this feel nice."

"Mabel doesn't have AC?"

"No, sir."

"Humph." The tall, slender man with a shock of white hair and an impressive handlebar mustache wandered to a sagging brown recliner. A massive Maine coon cat took up the entire seat. He hefted it up to toss onto the sofa, then settled into his chair. "Have a seat."

The offended cat glared before starting a tongue bath.

Effie chose a simple oak rocker, unsure how to broach the matter that had brought her here.

"How is Mabel? I trust she's okay?" Interesting. Far from being the monster Mabel had portrayed, Wallace seemed cordial enough—at least once he'd confirmed she wasn't witnessing or selling unwanted items.

"She's good."

"Does she talk much about me?" He leaned forward. "The last time we met at the Grange Hall, we'd both had a few spirits and I'm afraid I may have said something to offend her."

"I'm sure not." So much for Mabel's claim to never imbibe. "In fact, she's the one who suggested I come over, to—"

"Does she want me to come for supper? I'm available most any night of the week. My grandson's living with me, so he'd probably enjoy a good meal, too. Lord knows, neither one of us cooks."

"Actually—" now Effie was leaning in "—would your grandson happen to be named Marsh?"

"Yes. Why?"

She forced a deep breath. "I'm not sure how to say this, but I was working on our roof when I spied a horse carrying a man slumped in his saddle. Making a long story short, the man's hand was a mess, and showed signs of having been snake bit. I called an ambulance, and paramedics took him into La Junta." She fished Marsh's wallet from her back pocket, along with his broken wedding ring. "He should be fine, but—"

"Take me to him." He stood, holding out his hands for his grandson's things.

"E-excuse me?" She gave him the two items.

"I don't drive, so you'll have to take me to him."

"Oh—sure. Have trouble seeing?"

"Hell, no." He'd already stood and took a black leather cowboy hat from a rack next to the front door. "I got so many damned speeding tickets that the law revoked my license. Don't get it back till next month."

THE ANGEL HAD RETURNED.

Marsh winced from the too-bright lights when he tried focusing on her. She sat quietly by his bedside, staring down at him as if he was no longer a man, but a museum exhibit.

We've administered forty-six units of antivenin. It's too soon to give an accurate prognosis of the probability of lasting damage.

That didn't sound good.

In fact, nothing sounded good except for the angel's soft, nonsensical hum. The tune soothed him in a way that he didn't understand, but welcomed.

His wife hadn't been in to see him, but his son had assumed a large role in Marsh's dreams.

The two of them played Frisbee with the dog and made sand castles on the beach. Tucker must not have drowned, because his smile reminded Marsh of his reason for living. His job as a SEAL was important, but being a dad was his life's true calling.

"Are you awake?" the angel asked.

"I—I think so?" His mouth was so dry that his tongue protested forming even the simple words. *Do you have water?* He might have asked the question, or maybe he'd only touched his lips?

"Thirsty? I'm not sure if you're allowed to have anything to drink. There was talk of you having surgery, but I'll go see." She stood, as if planning to leave.

"No," he said. "Stay."

"I'll be right back. Let me find a nurse."

"Stay. Meet my son." He locked his gaze with hers and more than anything, he needed that connection. Everything was messed up in his head. But if she promised not to leave him, he just might be okay.

EFFIE TIGHTENED HER grip on the ICU waiting room's courtesy phone. After Effie had explained that their mystery man was Wallace's grandson, Mabel asked about Marsh's condition.

"Wish I had better news to report, but he's still pretty out of it."

"What does his doctor say?"

"Nothing specific. He's not in danger of dying, but his hand's in bad shape."

"I'll say more prayers for him. You stay as long as you need. The kids are all fine."

"Thank you for watching them. Since Wallace lost his license due to a few too many speeding tickets, I don't feel right leaving either of them."

"You're right to stay with Marsh. The poor soul's grandfather might be a heathen, but that doesn't mean he's guilty by association."

After chatting with Remington for a few minutes—Colt still wasn't talking to her—Effie hung up and wandered her way back to Marsh's room.

Poor Wallace. The man had been downgraded from scoundrel to heathen.

She froze outside Marsh's room, hesitant to interrupt his lovable grandfather, who sat near the head of the bed. The last of the day's sun filtered through generous windows, softening the harsh reality of Marsh's grim situation.

Where was the man's wife? The son he'd earlier mentioned?

A machine beeped in time with Marsh's painfully slow pulse. His bed was surrounded by IVs pumping him full of fluids and different medicines. His handsome features twitched from the venom. The sight broke her heart, yet she couldn't look away. Hash marks had been drawn up his arm to show how far the poison advanced.

Maybe because she'd been the one to find him, Effie felt an inexplicable connection to the man. A fierce protective streak made her irrationally angry at his wife, who should have been by his side.

Unable to remain silent, she approached Wallace. "If you have contact information, I don't mind calling Marsh's wife. I'm sure having his family here would be a comfort."

"You're a sweet gal, but it might be best for you to steer clear of messy family business."

"Oh. Okay." The cramped room only had one chair, so she leaned against the far wall, trying to make sense of Wallace's cryptic words. *Messy family business?* She'd experienced more than her fair share of that. Were Marsh and his wife divorced? Had his ex been given sole custody of their son?

As bothersome as her boys could sometimes be, Effie couldn't imagine a life without her children.

"On second thought…" Wallace grunted before leaning hard on the armrests to rise from his blue vinyl chair. "Show me the way to a cup of strong black coffee and I'll get your take on the matter."

"There's coffee in the waiting room, but it's fresher in the cafeteria. Plus, they have surprisingly good sandwiches." Why couldn't she stop rambling? How had

Marsh Langtree grown to matter so much in such a short time?

She took a lingering glance at him before letting Wallace lead her from the room.

At eight thirty on a Monday night, the sandwich selection was slim, but Effie found a turkey on rye and Wallace opted for ham and Swiss, along with a piece of banana cream pie.

He insisted on paying for both of their meals, then showed her to a corner table.

They both ate in silence punctuated by faint metallic bangs and trays clattering in the kitchen. The antiseptic smell on the ICU wing had been replaced by the more pleasant aroma of fresh-brewed coffee.

Hospital employees came and went. The only other patient visitors in the dining area were a family Effie recognized from the ICU waiting room. The father had suffered a heart attack, but his prognosis was good.

Wallace had only eaten a third of his sandwich when he changed course to attack his pie. He finished in four bites, then washed it down with half his cup of joe. "That's better." He wiped pie crumbs from his mustache. "Now, I suppose this is something best kept in the family, but I would appreciate a woman's take on the matter."

"Of course." Effie leaned in.

"Let me first say I'm no angel. What seems like a hundred years ago, I made a killing in oil. I let the money go to my head, stepped out on my wife, and she packed up our little girl and left me. Marsh is my daughter Jacinda's son. I only cheated that one time, and I was so damned drunk I didn't remember much other than waking up with a head throbbing with regret, but my wife wasn't having it, and she moved back out east to stay with her folks. They were a hoity-toity bunch who dabbled in Thoroughbred breeding and never much cottoned to me. We were separated for forty years before Jacinda called to tell me her mama died from flu." He shook his head while tears shone in his eyes. "Flu. You hear about folks dyin' from it on the news, but it seems like an unnecessary way to go."

"I'm sorry." Effie placed her hand over Wallace's.

He snatched his hand back and waved off her concern. "No need for sympathy. The damned fool woman made her choices, same as me. Save for ten minutes, I was faithful to her my whole life, but got nothin' to show for it. Now, I finally have my grandson with me, and look what happened to him."

"You could no more control Marsh getting bit by a rattler than you could the outcome of your infidelity. Sometimes life just plain sucks."

He snorted and reached for his fork, pressing crumbs between the tines. "What's worse, my grandson's now in the same kind of bind."

"Marsh cheated on his wife?" Effie's respect for him plummeted.

"No, no. Of course, not. Hell, they've been divorced for darn near three years, and he still wore his ring—took a rattler to pry it off him. I just meant that he's as alone as I am. When his little boy drowned, Jacinda worried grief might drive Marsh under."

Wallace's story trapped Effie's heart on a spinning carnival ride. Up and down, around and around. Whereas moments earlier, she'd felt contempt for the man, she now ached for him. Had his wife blamed him for the loss of their son? And was that why their marriage died, too?

She drew her lower lip into her mouth. Poor, poor Marsh.

"I didn't share all of this to draw pity. I don't get out much, and am genuinely curious to hear a woman's point of view. Was my wife right to never speak to me again? Was Marsh's wife right to leave him?"

Effie slowly exhaled. "Honestly, without hearing both sides, it's hard to say. But just having heard your version, sounds like you and Marsh both deserved another chance."

Silent tears streamed down the man's weathered cheeks.

He wadded his napkin, turning his back to her while drying his eyes. "I'm a silly old fool."

She rose to hug him. "It's never wrong to love someone, and it sounds to me like you and your grandson loved your wives very much."

Achy longing took hold in Effie's gut.

More than anything, all she'd ever wanted besides being a nurse was to be a great mom and to be loved. Love seemed like such a simple thing. Lots of people had it. What was it about her that Moody had found so unlovable?

Would any guy find her worthy of his affection?

She chided herself for even asking the question. With three kids and a grandmother and ragtag ranch to tend, the last thing she had time to even think about was a man.

Chapter Three

Marsh woke to bright sun, cartoons and fighting. Since none of that made sense, he closed his eyes, figuring when he next woke, life would once again be normal.

Give it!

No!

Yes!

Boys!

Something broke.

Both of you sit down. If I have to tell you again, you're not going to Scotty's party.

I hate you! I'm calling Dad!

Colt William Washington! This voice was different—older sounding, in a scolding, grandmotherly way.

Grandma, I'm sorry. I thought the boys would behave, but—

"Hey…" Marsh fully opened his eyes to find not one boy who would have been older than Tucker when he'd passed, but two. "How come you're giving your mom such a hard time?"

"You're awake!" A petite blonde rushed to his side. *My angel?* He recalled the sweetest humming and soft strokes to his hair. She clapped her hands to flushed cheeks, then her hair, then to his shoulder. "Oh my gosh. I need to get your grandpa. He's going to be so happy."

One of the boys stepped alongside his mom. "Your hand blew up to the size of a football and had lots of icky gunk squirting out of it. It was *awesome!*"

Not to be outdone, a clone of the first boy said, "When I was little, a stick poked out my eyeball!"

"Remington, Colt, come here." The grandmotherly voice was attached to a slim body with spiky white hair. "Leave that poor man alone."

Marsh licked his lips. "Would one of y'all mind helping me out with a few clues as to what's going on?"

The boy scampered to a window seat, where he joined his other half in coloring in a Transformers book with crayons.

"I'm sorry." The angel's flighty hands were back to her cheeks. "I'm Effie. You were bitten by a rattler, and I found you and your horse. These little hellions are my boys—Colt and Remington. And this—" she put her arm around the older woman who had her impish smile "—is Mabel. My saint of a grandmother, who took us all in."

Mabel said, "We're your grandfather's neighbors to the east."

"Guess I owe you a heap of gratitude." Marsh struggled just to scratch his stubble-covered jaw. "Everything that happened is kind of a blur." *Mostly what I remember is you, Effie. The way you made me want to fight my way back from the dark.*

A crying whimper came from somewhere near the window.

His angel headed that way to pluck an infant from a carrier. With a cherub-cheeked mini version of herself, only with curls, settled on her hip, Effie returned. "This is Cassidy. She gets cranky when she's left out of the action."

"Don't blame her." Marsh tried reaching for the nearest of the infant's bare feet, but even that small effort seemed too great. The sensation of not being in control of his body was not only unfamiliar, but intolerable.

He needed out of this bed *now*.

"You probably shouldn't try to do too much at once."

"Lifting my arm is hardly too much."

"I'll be damned…" His grandfather took off his cowboy hat while entering the cramped room. "You lived."

"Don't have to sound so excited about it."

His granddad chuckled. "Believe you me, I am. If something happened to you while you were out here, your mama would have my hide."

"True." For as long as Marsh could remember, Wallace had been part of his life. He called every Sunday morning and sent him cash-filled cards for holidays with extra on his birthdays. When Marsh's perfect family had officially gone to hell, and his CO told him to get his head on straight and not even think about coming back until he'd made peace with his son's passing and his wife leaving, the only place that made sense for him to go was to the ranch where he'd spent every childhood and teen summer. His maternal grandmother's Thoroughbred farm where he'd grown up was home, but about as regimented as his Navy schedule. What he needed was plenty of time and wide-open spaces to make sense out of the mess that had become of his life. "Have you talked to Mom? Told her I'll be all right?"

Wallace nodded. "She wanted to fly out, but I told her you didn't need a woman interfering in your business."

"Sounds like something you'd say." Mabel crossed her arms, and a slash replaced her pretty smile.

"Thank you for proving my point," his grandfather snapped before slapping his hat back on his head.

Never had Marsh wished more for the strength to form

a simple time-out T with his hands. After the two septuagenarians bickered for another five minutes, he glanced toward Effie and caught her gaze.

She smiled.

His chest tightened when they shared a moment of mutual frustration with their elders.

"Gramma?" One of the boys had left his coloring book to cock his head and stare up at her. "How come you tell me and Colt not to fight, but you and Mr. Wallace fight, too?"

Marsh didn't even try hiding a smile.

Effie squeezed her son's shoulder, steering him toward the door. "Colt, would you please pack up your coloring books and crayons, then grab Cassidy's carrier. We should probably go."

"Agreed." Mabel glared toward Marsh's grandfather. "I need out of here before this darn fool goes and tells me again that I'm shakin' like a wet dog."

"You're still holding a grudge about that?" Wallace asked.

Effie winced. "Remington, please help your brother put those crayons back in the box."

"Woman…" Wallace made the mistake of pointing his finger in Mabel's face. She looked angry enough that Marsh wouldn't have put it past her to break his grandpa's finger clear off. "What in the world are you talking about?"

"Oh—now, you're going to fake amnesia? My poor Dwayne had barely been in his grave a year, and I was finally able to get back to square dancing. You blustered into the regular Saturday night party and sauntered up to me without even taking off your hat. Then you said those horrible words, and Wallace Stokes, I've hated you ever since."

"Hated me? I said you shook like a dog as a compliment. I used to have an old hound named Peacock, and I loved that girl something fierce. Nothing made me happier than taking her down to the swimming hole and watching her play in the water, and then shake off. Made me smile—truly. Just like your dancing." He removed his big black cowboy hat, pressing it to his chest while making the strangest smile. "Miss Mabel, from the bottom of my heart, I give you my deepest, most sincere apology."

Mabel shook her head. "Boys, hurry along before we all suffocate from Mr. Stokes's bloviating hot air."

"Grandma." Effie shifted her baby to her other hip. "Wallace said he was sorry. After hearing his explanation, don't you think this is all sort of funny?"

Marsh yawned. "I don't mean to interfere in anyone's business, but I sure could use a nap."

"Aw, now, I'm sorry," Effie said to him. "Boys, Grandma—let's go."

"Gladly." Mabel huffed and headed toward the door.

The boys marched behind her, as did Wallace, smooth talking all the way out into the hall.

When only Effie remained, she said, "I really am sorry. After what you've been through, you should have woken to a nice, peaceful scene."

"It's all right." He cast her a faint smile. "Guess I'm lucky to even be alive." Which surprised him. At what point had he decided living was better than dying?

"You sure are." She came close enough to cup her hand to his shoulder. Her simple, kind touch flooded him with a sense of calm and well-being. "Since my crew isn't exactly suitable for hospital visits, now that you're awake, I probably won't be back."

"Sure. I understand." Only he didn't. Why did he suddenly want more than anything to see her and her wild brood again? "Thanks for the time you were here—and for calling an ambulance for my pitiful behind."

"It was my pleasure." When she smiled, the pleasure was all his.

"THAT MUST HAVE been horrible."

"It was," Effie said.

It was Sunday afternoon, and while the twins splashed in Scotty's pool, Effie sat at the back porch table with Cassidy asleep on her lap. Scotty's mother, Patricia, and three other moms she'd just met whose names she couldn't remember had shared Little League gossip until the conversation turned to Marsh's snakebite ordeal, whose injury made the local paper.

"Will he regain full use of his hand?" one of the moms asked. She had big hair and wore an equally large purple sundress patterned with cows jumping over pink moons.

"Hope so." Effie wished she knew what was going on with Marsh. Had he been released? It seemed strange that she'd spent so much time with him when he'd been unconscious, yet now that he was awake, she hadn't seen him at all. How could she miss him when she didn't even know him?

The conversation wound to the upcoming school year that officially started in the morning. Effie excused herself to grab the boys from the pool. With all the excitement over Marsh, she hadn't even started shopping for their supplies.

Rounding the edge of the free-form pool, she couldn't help but notice how luxurious Patricia's home was. Scotty's father, Roy, was a lawyer, and had spent more time on his cell phone than playing with the boys, but now he'd joined his wife on the porch. They shared a kiss, and when he whispered something for only her to hear, Effie fought a jealous pang.

She didn't miss Moody, per se, but she missed the intimacy of being a couple. Of knowing no matter what curves life threw her way, he had her back. Only in the end, he hadn't. The fact still kept her up nights, and when the boys acted out, it made her more convinced than ever that they needed a firm masculine presence in their lives.

Effie turned from the happy couple to summon her boys.

The pool had been constructed to resemble a country pond. A pile of boulders at the deep end featured a grotto with a swim-up bar and slide. Country music played from speakers hidden in more rocks, and the sweet scent of petunias blended with suntan lotion and chlorine and lingering smoke from the grill to form the perfect backdrop for a lazy summer afternoon.

"Colt! Remington!" she called above the splashing, shifting Cassidy to her other hip. "We need to go!"

"No!" Colt swooshed his hand through the water, creating a massive wave. "We're having fun!"

"Now." Effie walked to the pool's edge. "If you're not out of this pool by the time I count to ten, you're grounded from TV and your friends for the whole first week of school."

Cassidy must have sensed the change in her mother's mood, as she whimpered. "It's okay, sweetie," Effie said with a light jiggle. "Mommy's not mad at you."

Remington sloshed to the pool's edge and hopped out, racing across the sandstone pavers for his towel.

"Don't run!" she shouted after him.

Meanwhile, Colt crossed his arms and glared. "I don't wanna go!"

"One." Why was Colt doing this? He never used to

talk back when Moody had been around. Was she such a horrible parent that she'd brought out this defiant streak?

He stood chest-deep in the water, staring.

"Two."

His friends stopped playing keep-away to gawk. Apparently the parental showdown was more entertaining?

"Three."

"Colt, come on," his brother said. "We gotta pick school stuff."

"No!" Colt looked away to swim to the deep end.

"Four." Effie's heart pounded. She'd always hated confrontations, and fighting with her son in such a public setting was the worst.

"I'll get him, Mom." Bless his little heart, Remington handed her his towel, jumped back in the pool, and swam to his brother. He whispered something in his ear, then Colt slapped the water but eventually turned for the shallow end.

"Thanks for your help," she said when Remington stood beside her while Colt took his time getting his Spider-Man towel.

"You're welcome."

She wanted to ask Remington what he'd said that had worked such magic but in the end realized she didn't want to know. What if her youngest boy had told his big brother that if he didn't come, Mom was going to have a stroke? Or embarrass them even more in front of their friends?

When Colt finally reached her, Cassidy's weight had taken a toll on Effie's lower back. Eager to place the baby in her car seat, she said to both boys, "Go and thank Mr. and Mrs. Crawford, then get dressed. We need to hurry and get to the store."

TWO HOURS LATER, frazzled didn't begin to cover Effie's mood. The school supplies had cost double what she'd budgeted and Colt had insisted on specialty items instead of plain number-two pencils and standard notebooks. She knew she should have told him no, but it was tough when Remington behaved like a saint in the crowded back-to-school aisle and deserved a little something special for the start of first grade.

She had money tucked away from selling vegetables and eggs at the summer farmer's market, and every so often Moody did send a check, but she hated needing his money and felt guilty living off Mabel's generosity. Effie vowed to one day finish nursing school so she'd be able to support herself.

Last year, Moody had been with her and the boys when they'd shopped for kindergarten supplies. When Colt pitched a fit over wanting the extra-large box of crayons with the built-in sharpener, Moody hefted him over his shoulder and carried him kicking and screaming to the truck.

Unsure what she'd do if Colt behaved like that with her, she'd bowed to his pressure—a horrible parenting move, but what else could she have done? With Cassidy riding in her carrier, if Colt pulled a stunt like running off, her only option would have been hefting his brother into the cart, then chasing after him.

Back at Mabel's ranch, Effie was surprised to find a familiar red Ford pickup in Mabel's drive. What was Wallace doing at the house? Had he driven himself without a license? More importantly, her racing pulse wondered, had he brought his grandson? If Marsh was even out of the hospital.

After parking her minivan, she flipped down the visor to check if she looked as bad as she felt—just in case

Marsh was feeling well enough to tag along. In a word? Yes. Her once-neat ponytail sagged, and dozens of wispy curls framed her flushed face.

"What'cha lookin' at, Mom?" Remington still sat in his safety seat, but Colt had already unbuckled himself and opened the van's side door.

Since she couldn't tell her son she was checking herself out for a possible encounter with the handsome neighbor, she crossed her fingers behind her back before saying, "I, um, thought I had something in my eye."

"Oh." He scrambled from his seat to take Cassidy from hers. "Ready to see Great-Gramma?" he asked his baby sister in an adorable soft tone.

Cassidy grinned, bucking with excitement.

"Sure you're strong enough to carry her?" Effie asked.

"Mo-om." He rolled his eyes. "I'm *really* big, and she's *really* small."

"Oh, well in that case, you can always carry her." She kept a close eye on the pair while opening the van's rear door. "How about you start by taking her in the house. Colt and I will grab your school supplies."

"Okay." He took his time with his baby sister, being extra careful on the short step to the porch.

"There you are." Mabel burst out the front door.

Wallace followed behind her, then spotted Effie. "Let me help with that. Looks like you've got your hands full."

He bounded out in front of Mabel to take Effie's bags.

"Thank you." She eyed her blushing grandmother, whose expression landed between the cat who swallowed a canary and a randy teen who'd been caught making out. "Everything all right?"

"Oh, fine, fine," Wallace said. "Marsh!" He waved toward the barn, where his grandson exited at a snail's pace. "Come on over here. You should both hear our happy news."

Mabel beamed.

What in the world is going on?

And how did any man have a right to look so good straight out of the hospital? Should he even be walking? Marsh's left hand was bandaged. He wore jeans and a white T-shirt with NAVY written on the front in big blue letters. She couldn't tell which was in worse condition, his battered cowboy boots or his equally shabby brown leather cowboy hat. The closer he got, the more she couldn't help but wonder how she hadn't before noticed his eyes being quite so dark. Like decadent fudge pools.

"Hi," she said with a painfully awkward wave in his direction, willing her runaway pulse to slow. "Should you already be up and around?"

"Judging by how crappy I'm feeling, nope." He winced. "But I needed to check on my horse. Thanks for taking care of him."

"It's been my pleasure. If you want, he can stay here till you feel up to riding."

"That'd be great. Thanks." His half smile turned her knees to rubber. Shame on her. As the single mom of three kids, the last thing she had time for was checking out a cowboy—especially one with even more emotional baggage than her.

"Did you kill the snake that bit you?" Colt asked.

"I did not," Marsh said.

"Aren't you mad at him?" Her son had already taken his new Batman backpack from the van and now wore it.

"Nah." Marsh ruffled the boy's hair the way Moody used to. "I figured he was just protecting his land the same way I would mine. Make sense?"

"I guess?" Colt cocked his head and frowned.

Wallace cleared his throat. "I don't mean to interrupt, but me and Miss Mabel have some mighty exciting news." He slipped his arm around her slim shoulders. "Don't we, darlin'?"

Mabel beamed. "We sure do."

Much as they had at the hospital when their grandparents had been fighting, Effie shared a look with Marsh. Was he as confused as she was?

"Look here." Marsh's grandfather took Mabel's hand, waving it for all to see. A massive diamond solitaire glinted in the setting sun. "Effie, honey, your gorgeous grandmother has agreed to marry me."

"What?" Effie pressed her hands to her galloping heart.

Marsh looked ready to topple over.

"You heard right," Mabel said. "We're getting married! And we want the two of you to be our best man and maid of honor."

Chapter Four

"Wait…" Marsh fought the temptation to conk the side of his head to check for something in his ear, because surely he hadn't heard right. "Did you just say you're getting *married*?"

"Isn't it exciting?" Effie's grandmother gushed. "And since neither of us is getting younger, we want to hold the ceremony right away—but with enough time to do it up right."

Her beaming groom slipped his arm around her waist and the two shared a kiss.

Lord…

Marsh sneaked a peek at Effie and found her looking as bewildered as he felt.

"Grandma," she said, "and Wallace, I'm thrilled for both of you—really, I am. But don't you think this is a little sudden? At the start of the week, you hated each other."

Wallace waved off her concern. "Like your grandmother said, at our age, there's no sense in putting off till tomorrow what should be done today."

"Mom?" One of the twins tugged the bottom of Effie's pretty floral shirt. "Do married people share beds? 'Cause my friend Scotty said—"

"Gosh, Colt." Effie clamped her hand over her son's

mouth and steered him toward the coop affixed to the side of the barn. "I'm pretty sure you and your brother forgot to feed the chickens this morning."

Remington thankfully followed.

Marsh struggled to hold back a laugh. But then he thought of his grandfather's upcoming honeymoon night and wanted to cry. How was it fair the old guy would soon be seeing more action than him?

"Ready to set our big date?" Wallace asked his bride.

"Absolutely." Mabel was already heading for the house. "I've got one of those big bank calendars on the side of the fridge."

"Perfect." Wallace took her hand to walk her into the house. It was a damn shame his grandmother had held tight to her grudge for so many years. Wallace clearly had an abundance of affection to share with no previous outlet. Maybe this marriage was a good thing after all?

"Quite a turn of events, huh?" Effie tucked her hands in the back pockets of faded jeans that hugged her in all the right places.

"No kidding." Marsh tried not to notice the strain her pose placed on her shirt's pearl buttons.

"How are you doing? Let's get you off your feet and out of the sun." She led him toward a bench in the barn's deep afternoon shadow.

"Better now." He hated feeling as if his normally strong body had betrayed him. Upon sitting, he released a long sigh. "Crazy, isn't it? How a critter no longer than my arm put me out of commission."

"If you think that's bad, don't mess with a brown recluse. When I was a nursing student—"

"Hold up—you're a nurse? No wonder you took such great care of me."

"No. Not quite." She leaned against the barn wall and

lowered her gaze. "I, ah, dropped out just before my last semester."

"That sucks. Not that it's any of my business, but why?"

"Long story. Let's just say I caught a bad case of bull rider fever that led to an even more serious condition called marriage."

"Uh-oh…" He nodded. "I can relate—only the other way around."

"I'm sorry. Wallace told me the highlights—or I guess that would be lowlights—of what happened. Sorry doesn't seem adequate." Initially, Marsh had been irked by the fact that his grandfather had shared his private pain with a stranger, but for the instant it took Effie to cover his hand with hers, and he glanced up to find her blue-green gaze shimmering, his annoyance faded into appreciation for this woman who'd done more for him in the past week than his ex had in the past three years.

"It's okay." He stretched his legs out in front of him and leaned back. "I mean, clearly, it's not, but you get the picture."

She nodded and swallowed hard. "I can't imagine losing your son. You must have—"

"Stop." He straightened. "That's not a part of my life I care to hash over, so could we change the subject?"

"Sure. Sorry. I never meant to—"

"Damn, it's hot out here." Since she apparently hadn't gotten his earlier memo, Marsh stood. "Wonder when this heat's going to let up?"

He made the mistake of looking her way, only to find her big blue eyes once again shining. *Swell.* If there was one thing he couldn't abide more than heat, it was a crying woman. Unable—or hell, maybe just plain unwilling—to make more small talk, he nodded toward her grandmother's ragtag house. "I'm gonna see what's keeping Wallace."

Instead of waiting for her to acknowledge his statement or even follow him, Marsh took off. Over the years, Wallace had done a lot of crazy things, but this engagement took the proverbial cake to a whole new level. Marsh was partially pleased as punch for the old coot, but another part of him knew if the planning constantly threw him and Effie together, the next weeks could be rough.

The whole reason he'd come Colorado was to avoid people. Since losing Tucker to drowning and then his wife to a spectacularly civil divorce, Marsh hadn't been himself. A few months after the ink had dried on their papers, he'd been in Afghanistan watching a terrorist cell. He'd witnessed them strapping a bomb around the chest of a boy who couldn't have been much older than his son and lost it. Marsh had been on a strict intel-gathering mission that soon turned into a bad-guy bloodbath. He'd come damn close to being court-martialed for failure to follow orders, but by God, that innocent child had survived. Reuniting him with his mother had been one of the few times since losing Tucker that Marsh had felt alive.

Now? Hell, most days he wasn't sure what he felt—if anything at all. Truth be told, that snakebite had been a blessing if only for the fact that it had shaved a chunk of time from his life when he hadn't had to think about what happened to his marriage and son.

THE NEXT MORNING, guilt churned Effie's belly, because she actually felt relieved and a trifle giddy about waving goodbye to her rowdy twins, who had just climbed on the school bus. It had been a long summer, and later, she looked forward to planting her behind on one of the front porch rockers to linger with Cassidy over a nice cup of tea.

And if her thoughts strayed to the proud, handsome, clearly heartbroken man to whom she would soon be related by marriage?

The unspoken question warmed her cheeks.

Well, there was certainly no harm in thinking about a person, was there? His story was beyond tragic, and lingered with her long after he and Wallace had gone. It had been hard enough losing her husband, but to have also lost a child? No wonder Marsh hadn't cared to talk about his situation, but the way he'd cut her off had been downright rude—especially when she'd only been trying to help.

She'd just entered the house to clean up the breakfast dishes when she spotted her grandmother not where she'd last been—at the kitchen table, feeding the baby pureed peaches—but emerging from her bedroom wearing her best Sunday dress and a huge smile.

Cassidy squealed while racing down the wood-floored hall in her walker, making an awful racket with the squeaky buttons and electronic horn.

So much for my quiet morning...

"How do I look?" Mabel performed a lively pirouette.

"Pretty as a picture. But where are you off to so early on a Monday morning?" She didn't drive, so one of her friends must be coming to get her.

"Did you already forget? When Wallace and Marsh were leaving, we decided to meet up for a planning breakfast at Mom's Café and then hit the ground running. Hurry up and get dressed. We're supposed to meet them in fifteen minutes."

"Grandma, you never said anything about seeing your *fiancé* today." Just saying the word sounded awkward, but not nearly as bad as spending a whole day with Marsh would be.

"I'm sure I did…" Mabel ducked into the hall bathroom to fluff her white hair. "Now, hurry. I don't want to be late."

"For the record, you must have been talking to angels, since you sure never ran any of this past me."

"Watch your sass, or I'll downgrade you from maid of honor to punch bowl attendant."

Effie rolled her eyes.

Under the best of circumstances, prepping Cassidy and all of her gear was never easy, but on short notice? The task was darn near impossible. By the time Effie swapped comfy jeans and a T-shirt for a sundress and wrestled the baby into a cute yellow gingham romper, her fifteen minutes had ticked to five. After loading the diaper bag, stroller, carrier and her purse in the back of the minivan, then plopping the baby into her safety seat, Effie was not only exhausted, but ten minutes off schedule.

She slid behind the wheel, relieved to have at least made it into the car.

"Couldn't you have at least tried doing something with your hair?" Mabel cast a dour glance in Effie's general direction. "I don't want Wallace thinking he's marrying into a bunch of hillbillies."

Overheated, Effie turned on the engine and AC before yanking down the visor to peer into the lighted mirror. Good grief. The ponytail she'd slept on hung sideways with more hair out than in. For added flavor, compliments of Colt, there was oatmeal just over her right ear. Effie said a quick prayer for his teacher, Mrs. Logan. She'd need all the help she could get to hog-tie him to his desk.

"Is this better?" Effie asked after yanking out her elastic, only to smooth her hair back and work it back in.

Mabel frowned. "I like it better down. And when you add a bit of curl. For sure wear it that way at the wedding. I don't want it looking bad for pictures."

It was official. Her normally sane grandmother had turned into Bridezilla.

"THERE'S MY BLUSHING BRIDE."

While Effie struggled into the crowded café with Cassidy on her hip and the diaper bag over her shoulder, Mabel glided to where her groom sat at a table loaded with rowdy geriatrics Effie recognized from the Grange Hall, where she drove her grandmother most Saturday nights. Funny how she hadn't noticed Wallace, too. Had Mabel deliberately kept her distance?

Mabel and Wallace shared a brief embrace and kiss, then he pulled out a chair for her alongside his.

"Hope you don't mind," he said to Effie, "but there's no more room here, so I figured you could sit with Marsh." He nodded to the room's far corner, where his grandson glowered over a mug of coffee.

Effie opened her mouth to tell him that as a matter of fact, she very much minded, but the group of three women and four men was too loud for her voice to have even been heard. Resigned to her fate, she lugged the baby a little farther.

As if the whole town was relieved school was back in session, honky-tonk played on the jukebox. Laughter and high-spirited conversations rose above the music. The scents of strong coffee and bacon and the café's famous cinnamon rolls had Effie's stomach growling.

"Are you as sick of this wedding as I am?" she asked upon reaching Marsh's table.

"Oh, hey. Yes." He jumped up to help her with Cassidy's bag. "Welcome to the kids' table. I wouldn't be surprised if the waitress shows up with a pair of smiley-face pancakes."

"I know, right?" The brief brush of the back of his hand against her shoulder had her fighting a flutter of awareness low in her belly. Gracious, he was a looker. He hadn't shaved, and if possible, when he politely removed his cowboy hat, his hair looked even worse than hers.

She'd always had a thing for untamed cowboys.

Case in point—her no-good ex.

Once she'd sat herself in a chair, her cell on the table and Cassidy on her lap, Marsh asked the waitress to bring a high chair, than slapped his hat back on.

"Thank you," Effie said, relieved to duck behind the laminated menu. When the waitress returned with the high chair, Effie hefted Cassidy in, then ordered hot tea and a cheese omelet with hash browns.

"Question," Marsh said once they were alone. "Do you remember hearing anything about this meeting yesterday afternoon?"

Laughing, Effie shook her head. "I walked my boys to the school bus, thinking Cassidy and I had the whole day to ourselves, only to learn I was wrong."

"Sorry." Marsh sipped his coffee.

"Why should you apologize? I assume you had better things to do this morning, too."

"True—no offense."

"None taken." She fished the baby's favorite rubber whale teething toy from the diaper bag and set it on the high chair's tray. "This engagement happened so fast. The wedding's the third week in October. My head is spinning."

The waitress came and went with her tea. Effie added plenty of sugar.

"What if we divide and conquer?"

Effie wrinkled her nose. "You mean like Mabel and I handle flowers and you and your grandfather tackle beer and wine?"

"Exactly." He leaned in. "You have no more time or desire to be around me than I have to be around you. This way, we make Wallace and Mabel happy without the two of us being miserable. Sound like a plan?"

"Sure."

The waitress arrived with their meals, and Effie dived in, closing her eyes while savoring the gooey cheese.

But upon glancing into Marsh's hooded, dead-sexy gaze only to realize she wasn't miserable, she swallowed and then froze. What had she just agreed to? It wasn't as if she craved seeing the guy, but now that she'd lugged Cassidy and her gear into the real world outside her grandmother's modest home, she recognized that along with the café's food being far tastier than her own, she'd been tapping her toe to the lively music. Her baby girl grinned from all the neighboring diners' waves and silly faces.

Marsh might have admitted he was miserable, but she was far from it. Breakfast out was actually kind of a fun treat.

As for the view across the table? *Whew...*

Even brooding, Marsh Langtree's chiseled features were ridiculously easy on the eyes. Proven by the fact that she wasn't the only woman staring. How could his wife have left him? He seemed like a stand-up guy. Why had the death of their son driven them apart instead of bringing them closer?

Her cell rang.

One glance at the caller ID snapped her from her thoughts—Admiral Byrd Elementary.

"Need to get that?" Marsh asked.

"Unfortunately." What had Colt done? Dipped a girl's

braids in paint? Freed the occupants of the teacher's hamster cage or ant farm? Effie steeled herself for the worst. "Hello?"

"Mrs. Washington? I'm sorry to bother you, but—" Effie recognized the voice of Samantha, the school office clerk.

"What did Colt do?"

Samantha laughed. "Actually, nothing. The twins' teacher just wanted me to see if you're available next Thursday for a brief field trip. The kids are learning about money, so they'll be walking to the bank at the end of our block. Mrs. Logan is desperate for volunteers."

"Please tell her I'd be happy to help." Effie released the breath she'd been holding.

"Perfect. I'll let her know."

Upon disconnecting, Effie couldn't help but smile.

"Good news?" Marsh asked.

"In a roundabout way." She skimmed her palm over Cassidy's soft blond curls. "My twins are a handful—well, mostly Colt. He's oldest by three minutes, and always in trouble. This school year couldn't have come at a better time, as I'm in sore need of a parental breather. Anyway, during kindergarten, I got far more calls than I would have liked from the boys' teacher, and with today being the first day of school, I saw the caller ID and assumed the worst."

"But everything's okay?" He held a bacon strip to his lips, causing her tummy to flutter. When he'd been in the hospital, she'd stared at him for hours at a time, but he'd always been asleep. Now that he was awake, it was tough not to notice even more—like the way a fraction of an inch up or down at the corners of his mouth made him look happy or sad or devilishly sexy.

"Yes." *Or was it?* Face flushed from her latest assessment of her companion, she focused on squirting ketchup on her hash browns. For the moment, her twins might have been behaving, but her overactive imagination certainly wasn't. It was high time she focused more on this wedding and less on the best man!

MARSH COULDN'T GET away from Effie and her cute-as-a-button baby fast enough. He'd paid the bill, and Effie was back on her phone, gabbing with someone about healthy school snacks, when the baby dropped her toy. In the moment, he found himself back on parental autopilot, reaching to the floor to get it, then dipping his napkin in his water to wipe the whale clean.

He returned it to Cassidy, and her smile filled him with the kind of awe and wonder he'd long ago had for his son. He never would have pegged himself for the kind of guy who liked kids, but not long into Tucker's brief life, Marsh found himself wholly consumed with his son. What he ate, what he wore, what toys he played with. Tucker had been his world, and when he died... Well, for all practical purposes, Marsh had, too.

Effie's crew was his first exposure to kids since Tucker's passing, and Marsh found the experience to be all at once heady and cruel. He'd caught himself sneaking peeks at little Cassidy's chubby pink cheeks and big blue eyes that matched her mama's. When he bent forward to return her toy, he'd caught a trace of her baby-lotion scent, which led him right back to Tucker's infant years, and to how much fun it had been to make boat noises while playing with his rubber fleet in the tub, then wrapping him in a big soft towel, lotioning him before adding a fresh diaper and PJs before rocking him and watching his wife, Leah, nurse before they'd tucked him into his crib.

Knowing he'd never again kiss his son good-night or play catch with him or watch him shriek at the beach while running from a crab was too much to bear.

He had to get out of there.

Away from Effie and her sweet baby girl and her talk about how relieved she was to have breathing room away from her boys when he'd have literally given anything for one more moment with his son.

In that instant, hearing Effie laugh over the fact that she was actually happy to be away from her kids filled him with irrational rage. Not with her, per se, but his particularly painful lot in life.

On autopilot, desperate for fresh air and the kind of quiet he could only find in the middle of nowhere, Marsh pushed back his chair, pressed his hat tighter on his head and left the diner and town.

Grief drove him to push his truck too fast, and back at his grandfather's ranch, he followed the same trend while four-wheeling to the old homestead.

Only when Marsh had well and truly driven to the end of his world did he allow himself badly needed release.

He screamed at God.

Cursed fate.

He broke down and cried and wished that damned snake had finished what he'd started. Most of all, Marsh wished for a moment's respite from the heartache stemming from being well and truly alone.

Chapter Five

"Effie May Washington," Mabel scolded. "What did you do?"

"Nothing."

Mabel planted her hands on her hips. "You had to have done something to make Marsh bolt out of here faster than a spooked horse."

"Did he at least have the courtesy to pay for your meal?" Wallace asked.

Effie nodded.

"Since Marsh ran off with his truck, Effie, looks like you're our official chauffeur."

Swell.

"No worries. We'll have fun." Forcing a smile, Effie took Cassidy from her high chair, then vowed the first time she saw Marsh again, she'd give him a piece of her mind.

BY ELEVEN, THE BABY was squirming from being held too long and Effie couldn't tell whether Wallace and Mabel were fighting for real over the flowers or having a brief lovers' quarrel.

Rainbow Bridge Floral was owned by the same family who owned the town's only funeral home, so the rentable wedding arches and casket displays didn't make for the most ideal ambience. At least the place smelled good, with its sweet mix of roses, freesia and carnations.

"If we hold the ceremony at Rock Chapel but the reception at the Grange Hall, then we'll have to decorate both places, which means double the cost," Mabel explained to her fiancé, whose cheeks had turned red.

"But, darlin', I already told you," he said, "I don't give two green figs about the money. I've got more money than time, and want to spend my money and time on you."

Mabel opened her mouth to form a fresh argument, but Wallace leaned in to kiss the fight right out of her.

Swoon.

As frustrating as this whole wedding business was, Effie couldn't help but be thrilled for her grandmother—even a bit jealous. Being a single mom had never been part of her grand plan. She was supposed to have had a rewarding nursing career before even thinking about starting a family, but that hadn't exactly worked out, either.

Gloria, their floral consultant, cleared her throat. "Since your choice of venues is decided, are we ready to get back to deciding between roses and chrysanthemums?"

"Mums," Mabel said with a firm nod. "Much more budget friendly."

"Roses," Wallace said with a firm smack of his hands against the planning table.

"What if I kind of like mums?" Mabel asked. "Especially for fall?"

"Then we'll have both. Would that make you happy?"

Mabel nodded, and then she and her groom-to-be started in again with their kissing. *Really?*

Effie couldn't remember the last time she'd been well and truly kissed—probably the night Cassidy had been conceived. The notion made her sad. She used to love a night spent smooching beneath the stars.

A flash of Marsh and his oh-so-kissable lips popped into her mind's eye, but she squashed that image the way she would have a picnic ant. When—if—she ever found a suitable man for her and father for her children, he needed to be a whole lot more dependable than a guy who couldn't even be bothered to stick around for the official end of a meal.

"SOME BEST MAN you turned out to be."

"Sorry." From his seat on the living room sofa, Marsh glanced up from the online article his team member Rowdy had forwarded on the escalation of piracy along the Ivory Coast. He was just in time to catch the full brunt of the furrow between his frowning grandfather's bushy white eyebrows.

As if sensing trouble, Rocket, the massive Maine coon Wallace had found on the side of the road as a kitten, leaped from Marsh's lap to dart under the sofa, only his gut was so big, his entire ass end, complete with whipping tail, stuck out.

"Sorry doesn't cut it." Wallace slammed the front door. "You embarrassed the hell out of me, and hurt that sweet little gal Effie's feelings."

"Did she say something?"

"Didn't have to." Wallace snorted before collapsing onto his recliner and pushing himself fully back. "Poor thing had disappointment written all over her pretty face."

"Hope she didn't use permanent ink." Marsh didn't bother looking up from his iPad. He already had his grandfather's crotchety expression locked in his head.

"You're not too old for me to put soap in your mouth."

Marsh rubbed his suddenly throbbing forehead. "Point of fact, I kind of am, and I'm sorry. Next time I see Effie, I'll apologize."

"No, you're gonna do it now. By the time this wedding rolls around, I want everybody feeling harmonious. Besides, I left my wallet in that ugly minivan those women drive, and not only do I want it back, but I want you to take Effie into town and have her pick out a nice new SUV—something big enough to hold me and my bride, plus all those cute rugrats. Don't care what it costs. Oh— and don't skimp on the bells and whistles. Be sure you get those fancy heated seats and some of those TVs in the seat backs for my new great-grandsons."

"Is that all?" Marsh raised his right eyebrow. Another tour in Afghanistan was starting to sound simpler than his current ranch life. "You do realize the nearest dealer with a rig that swanky is gonna be in Colorado Springs?"

"I don't care if you have to drive all the way to Denver, just bring back that girl's smile or else." He signaled the conversation's end by using the remote to flip on his giant TV. The old guy loved *Let's Make a Deal*.

After setting his iPad on the coffee table, Marsh fished Rocket out from his hidey-hole to plop him back on the sofa, then trudged to the kitchen, where he'd left his truck keys.

Honestly, even if Wallace hadn't been adamant about Marsh apologizing, he'd planned on it anyway. Leaving Effie in the lurch hadn't been cool.

On the way to her and Mabel's place, he got stuck behind a school bus. This far out on their dead-end road, it no doubt carried Effie's sons.

Strange, but being around them hadn't dredged up the same stinging frustration that spending time with Effie's baby girl had. Maybe because Tucker had died so young,

Marsh hadn't had the privilege of seeing him at the stage where Colt and Remington now were.

He hung back—not just to avoid the dust cloud the vehicle raised on the dirt road, but to gain time to gather his composure.

What happened at breakfast wasn't just out of character for him, but one more indicator that his CO had been right in casting him off on extended leave. His head was in a bad place. But while there were all kinds of facilities and doctors he could have turned to for help with medical issues or PTSD, what was a guy supposed to do to cure the heartbreak of losing a kid? Oddly enough, he wasn't even that upset about his divorce. What did that mean?

When the bus stopped at the end of Mabel's drive and the boys shot off the vehicle in a sprint to the house, Marsh pulled the truck onto the road's weed-choked shoulder. And then he watched as Effie, with her adorable baby riding her hip, burst out the screen door to meet her twins. Clearly eager to talk about their first day back to school, the boys bounced like a couple of springs.

Effie's smile was big enough to see from fifty yards.

But then she raised her hand to her forehead, blocking her gaze from the sun. Understandably, upon seeing him, her happy expression faded.

Shit. Not that he much cared about losing her favor, but considering how much they'd be forced together till after the wedding, it made sense to keep the peace.

What didn't make sense was the fact that a long-buried part of him craved bringing back her smile.

On edge about a possible confrontation, Marsh's pulse hammered uncomfortably when the bus left, giving him the space needed to aim his truck down the drive.

By the time he parked, both boys raced to greet him. Marsh opened his door slow enough not to accidentally give one of them a conk, then grabbed his trusty cowboy hat from the passenger seat to plant on his head. The heat was intense, and he welcomed the shade.

"Guess what?" asked the twin in a red T-shirt with Spider-Man on it.

"We got hamsters in our school room and the dad ate his baby!" The other twin, wearing a blue T-shirt with the same character, beat his brother to the epic story.

"Yeah, and Miz Logan got all pinchy faced and told us to go to the reading corner, but I wanted to see, so I just stayed even though we weren't supposed to."

"Colt got a time out, and a poor choice *X* on Miz Logan's chart. He's in *big* trouble and gots a note for Mom to sign."

"*Has* a note for me to sign." Effie had slowly walked their way. "Marsh. I'll bet you're here for Wallace's wallet. Grandma just found it." Her words might have been friendly enough, but her expression wasn't. The boys' teacher wasn't the only "pinchy faced" woman in town.

"Right. He sent me to get it. Plus, I owe you an apology for what happened this morning."

"I'm okay." She jiggled the baby.

"I'm glad, but seriously, I'm sorry to have run out on you like that, and it won't happen again."

She shrugged.

"Hey!" A grubby hand tugged the hem of Marsh's black T-shirt. "There was blood in the hamster cage, and Miz Logan got sick-looking and called the janitor to clean it. He said that wasn't in his job *disk-kiption*, but he took it anyway, and then brought it back all clean."

"Colt…" Effie said in the universal mom warning tone. "Why don't you and your brother start on your chores, then we'll do homework."

"Don't have any!"

"Liar!" his twin said. "We've got math and a word find!"

"You're a tattletale!" The kid in the red shirt that Marsh assumed was Colt grabbed a fistful of dirt and chucked it at his brother.

"Ouch! You hit my eyeball!" The kid who had to be Remington by default started crying.

"Colt," Effie barked, "go to your room."

Cassidy's eyes welled as if she wasn't sure what to make of the situation.

"Mommy, my eyeball fell out!" Effie's youngest son clamped his hand over his left eye.

"Aw, honey." She looked to him, her huffing daughter, then Marsh. "Would you mind?" She held out the baby to him.

"Not a good idea." Backing away with his hands up, he added, "I've got germs."

She waved off his concerns and thrust her crying infant into his arms. "By the time you get to your third kid, you kinda give up on the whole germ thing."

Of course, Marsh grabbed hold of Cassidy or she might have fallen, but that landed him in the untenable position of feeling as if *he* were falling. The baby smelled so good and pure. And then there was pretty Effie wrapping her son in an invisible quilt made of love. Had fate not taken everything, this might be his life. Tucker would easily be old enough to have had a baby sister, and his ex had been great with their son.

"See, silly?" Effie pried Remington's hand finger by finger to get him to move it. "Your eyeball is not only still there, but I'll bet it works just fine. Want to check and see?"

"I don't know..." He sniffed and his bottom lip quivered. "It's *really* broken."

"Holy heck," Marsh shouted, "Remington, watch out for the lion!"

"What? Where?" The little boy removed his hand and opened his eye to look. "There's no lion."

"Sorry, bud. Guess my eyes might be broken, too, because that bush sure looked like a great big lion to me."

"It's okay." Remington played with the beads on his mother's necklace. "I sometimes get confused, too."

"But hey, at least your eyeball works, right?" Marsh kept a firm hold on the baby while crouching to give the little guy a high five.

"Wow, it does! Cool!" He turned to Effie. "Mom? Do we have any of that banana pudding Great-Gramma made?"

"Sure, babe." She ruffled his dark hair. "Help yourself. It's in the fridge." Once he'd scampered onto the porch and creaked open the screen door only to let it fall shut with a bang, Effie said, "Whew. Crisis averted. If I had a nickel for every time that kid has lost his eyeball..."

Marsh chuckled. "Kids are funny. My guy used to have a thing for Band-Aids. I swear a fly could land on his arm and he'd need it covered."

Instead of laughing, Effie's eyes shimmered. "Is this hard for you? Being around kids? At the restaurant this morning, I didn't even think about the fact that being around Cass might be rough."

"I'm good." Cool Marsh, in-control Marsh, the guy he wanted everyone to see, shrugged off her concern. But inside, her words soothed like the ointments and creams Tucker had always wanted along with his bandages. It had been a while since anyone had given a second thought to what he might be feeling. Hell, before his breakdown that morning, he'd begun to doubt he even still had feelings. Turned out he did, and instead of being short with her as he had when she'd first broached the subject of his son, this time around, the notion that his angel still cared touched him. "Want Cassidy?"

"If you don't mind, my back would appreciate leaving her right where she is. Besides, she looks awfully content. Hope that's not one of your favorite shirts?" She pointed to the SEAL insignia on the T-shirt's chest pocket.

Marsh glanced down to find the baby gumming the fabric while cooing. Drool formed a wet spot, and honestly, for a split second, the sensation felt like the normal operating procedure with Tucker. But then reality struck when he remembered time travel hadn't yet been invented and this baby wasn't even a boy, let alone his son.

"Thanks for that lion trick." Effie cocked her head in a way that had her long golden ponytail catching glints of afternoon sun—not that Marsh cared. It was just an observation.

Kind of like the way that necklace her son had been messing with had settled into that sweat-glistening hollow at the base of her throat?

Marsh cleared his throat, then, when the baby reached for his hat brim, passed her back to her mom. "Think she misses you."

Effie took her daughter, but she also took an extra long look at him that left him wondering if she hadn't zeroed in on exactly why he no longer wanted to hold the perfectly content child. Because no matter how loud he raged or how long he cried, being around kids just plain hurt.

"Come on inside, and I'll give you your grandfather's wallet."

"Sure." Feeling like an old hound, Marsh trailed after her, hating himself for checking out her behind in faded jeans that hugged her curves as well as any wet suit.

"Marsh. What a nice surprise." Mabel stood at the

stove, seeming unaffected by the afternoon heat. "When I found Wallace's wallet, I wondered how long it would take him to figure out it was gone." Whatever she had simmering smelled delicious—especially since he'd skipped lunch. From what little he knew about Mabel, all it would take for a dinner invite would be wielding his best smile, but the thought of sharing a table with not just the baby but the whole family was enough to send him running.

"Here you go." Effie handed him what he'd come for. "We only took half the cash." She winked.

"Actually, the old coot said he wants me to take you to buy a new ride. Said he didn't think your van would be big enough for the whole family once he and Mabel get hitched."

"That's crazy. You tell your grandfather thanks, but no, thanks. Me and that van lasted longer than my marriage."

"Will do." He slipped the wallet in his back pocket, tipped his hat to both ladies and turned for the door.

"Wait!" Mabel called. "Since you're here, you might as well stay for dinner. We usually eat early, on account of the kids needing to get to bed between seven and eight."

"That's a mighty kind offer," Marsh said, "but I just ate. I sure would have rather had something homemade."

"I understand. For sure, you come eat with us another time—in fact, anytime. Pretty soon, we'll be family and both you and your grandpa could use fattening up."

"Probably so, ma'am." After a last tip of his hat, Marsh bolted for the door before his starving stomach ratted him out by growling.

On the ride home, he wished for a logical answer as to why he'd outright lied to the kindly old woman, but the only thing he could come up with was the fact that out of all the hand-to-hand combat situations and gunfights and gnarly near-catastrophic water-based events he'd survived, nothing scared him more than being around Effie and her three kids.

Nothing had brought him deeper satisfaction than being a family man, yet never again would he open his heart to that kind of love. Why? Because it hurt too damned bad to lose it.

Chapter Six

"He scrambled out of here faster than a cat with its tail on fire." Mabel flipped the pork chops she was frying.

Taking salad fixings from the fridge, Effie said, "I think it hurts him—being around the kids."

"Why?"

"Wallace didn't tell you?" Effie normally wasn't one to gossip, but this was information Mabel kind of needed to know.

"Apparently not." She turned down the stove, covered the cast-iron skillet and wiped her hands on a dish towel.

"Marsh's three-year-old son drowned. Not long after, he and his wife divorced."

"Oh, dear…" Mabel clamped her hands over her mouth. "That's awful."

"I know. Outside, he apologized for running out on breakfast. He never came right out and explained why, but I'm guessing being around Cassidy brought back too many memories of his son."

"Maybe so…"

"Can I come out now?" Colt shouted from his room.

Effie sighed. "I forgot all about him being under house arrest."

"What did he do?" Mabel sat at the table.

Effie retold the day's events.

Mabel whistled. "That boy is a pistol. It's a darned shame Marsh wants no part of being around your boys. They sure could use a strong man in their lives."

"They're doing fine," Effie said, a bit harsher than she'd have liked. It irked her to no end when her grandmother inferred Effie wasn't doing an adequate job with the boys. Of course they needed their father, but what was she supposed to do about it? She couldn't remember the last time Moody sent a card, let alone called or stopped by for a visit. If she felt abandoned, it shouldn't come as too big of a surprise that his sons did, too. Only instead of internalizing their pain the way she did, they acted out—or at least Colt did. For the most part, Remington was a sweetheart. Poor Cassidy had been too young to even miss having a dad. Effie and Mabel and her brothers were the only family she'd ever known. "At least they'll all soon have Wallace—unless you want your privacy. I'd understand if you two want your own place, and I'll start looking for an apartment."

"Actually—" Mabel patted the table beside her "—have a seat. I wanted to wait until after the wedding to bring this up, but I figure now is as good a time as any."

"Okay…" *Should I be worried?*

Effie settled Cassidy in her walker, then joined her grandmother. "What's up?"

"I know this isn't the most pleasant of topics, but I'm not getting younger, and before I die, I want to—"

"Whoa." Effie held up her hands. "You're not sick, are you? And even if you are, we'll find—"

"Hush. I'm fine. We need to discuss my will—or, I guess the fact that there's no real need for one. Since I plan on leaving everything I own to you, and Wallace wants to do a bit of traveling, I figured why not deed it all over now? That way, after the wedding, you and the kiddos will still be settled here, and wherever Wallace and I decide to roam, I'll be worry free."

"Grandma, no. I couldn't." A peach-size knot lurked at the back of Effie's throat. "This is your house. I told you when we first came to stay that our being here was only temporary. You and Wallace hardly know each other. God forbid, what if things don't work out?"

"Then I assume you'd let me have my room back." Mabel laughed. "Child, Wallace and I have been carrying on quite the flirtation for years. The two of us feel right. Like a couple of old boots that finally got made into a pair. Now, let me have my way on this, and once my lawyer draws up the paperwork, I want you to sign. Okay?"

With her throat too tight to speak, Effie nodded.

"And get that awful look off your pretty face. This is a good thing. I just gave you a house and a leaky old barn. You should be thrilled."

Effie laughed through her tears. "That's the truth. Last time it rained, I'm pretty sure it was wetter inside the barn than out." She wrapped her grandmother in a fierce hug. "Thank you. For as long as I can remember, you've always been here for me. I appreciate you more than you could ever know."

"The feeling's mutual." Mabel kissed her cheek before checking on the pork chops. "Now, while I finish dinner, you might want to check on your three little devils. It's awfully quiet…"

True! Effie lurched from her chair to find the twins in the nursery. Cassidy grinned up at them from the floor, though if she'd had any idea what the two menaces were up to, Effie doubted she'd be amused. Colt held the mop, and Remington struggled to keep hold of a soapy, water-filled bucket they must have filled in the bathtub.

"What are you doing?" Effie took the bucket from her son before it sloshed all over the baby and the carpet.

"She has a dirty diaper," Colt said.

"We knew you was busy talkin' to Gramma, so we was gonna change it."

"We *were going to* change it. And thank you, but if you wanted to help, why not use a diaper wipe?"

"Eeeeew." The boys made matching disgusted faces.

"Mom," Colt said. "We didn't want to touch the poop. So we were going to mop it."

Effie took the mop, too. "I'll give you both points for creativity, but once I put these back in the closet, we're going to have a lesson on the right way to change your sister."

"Aw," Colt complained. "Do we have to?"

"Yes."

"I'm *not* touching poop." He crossed his arms.

Effie sighed. Now was one of those times when she wished for a strong male influence in the boys' lives. But she'd already loved and been left. Her heart couldn't take that kind of pain all over again, and she certainly wouldn't take a chance on subjecting her kids to it. Which left her on her own once Mabel and Wallace took off on their grand adventure.

Maybe Marsh would stay on at Wallace's ranch? If so, he'd had such a great touch with Remington. What if she offered to muck his horse stalls or something in exchange for him spending time with the boys? It would be embarrassing to even ask, but Moody had flat-out told her he had no time to help with the boys. When it came to Colt, she needed to be proactive before his behavior moved from being comical or bratty to downright dangerous—to either himself or others.

THREE DAYS LATER, the last place Marsh wanted to be was at a caterer's with the happy couple, Effie and her baby girl, but at least the food two perky gals kept bringing out tasted a helluva lot better than what he or Wallace got from opening a can.

Their tasting room had been set up in the former drugstore on the main drag through town. Maysville had a population of a few thousand on any given Saturday, but during the week, not much was going on. Horn Avenue was a four-block business district just off the two-lane highway leading to Colorado Springs. Ragtag businesses ranging from the café and feed store to a couple of bars and auto mechanics were bookended by two city parks. Cottonwoods and weeds were about the only things to grow, but a while back, the city council arranged through the Air Force Academy to have a pair of retired fighter planes installed alongside playgrounds.

The town's most impressive feature was its front-range Rocky Mountain view. On a clear day, Marsh felt as if he could see clear to heaven, which brought him closer to his son.

The four adults sat lined up at the old soda fountain while Cassidy sat on the floor in her carrier, cooing and batting at dangly toys.

Damn, she was a cutie.

So was her mom.

The heat hadn't let up, and Effie had knotted her long hair into a bun, only more hair seemed to have escaped than stayed up. She looked too thin, hot and frazzled—but real pretty. He had the craziest urge to whisk her off to a well-air-conditioned steak house to put meat on her bones.

"I'm partial to the prime rib." Wallace scowled at the portion of plain grilled chicken breast that Cherry of Cherry and Berry's Catering set in front of him. "I've never been a fan of much that walks on two legs." He turned to Mabel. "Except for you, sweet darlin'." Kiss, kiss.

"Aw, thank you, sweetheart. You're my favorite two-legged critter, too."

Marsh and Effie shared at look.

The happy couple had been at this for a good hour, and if a decision wasn't made soon, he was damn near ready to bolt—only this time he'd take Effie and Cassidy along for the ride. The lovebirds could fend for themselves.

Cherry noted the selection on her iPad. "So let's see. We've got the T-bone, prime rib and lobster for the buffet's meats. Ready to get started on the side dishes?"

Marsh raised his hand. "Mind if we take a break? I need to stretch my legs."

"Me, too." Effie was already standing.

"How about you two take a quick walk?" Mabel said. "I'll keep an eye on the munchkin."

"Thanks."

Marsh waited by the door while Effie gave her grandmother a sideways hug. Once they were outside, he asked, "What time do your boys get out of school?"

"Three fifteen."

"Damn. I was hoping it was earlier so you and Mabel would have an excuse to stop this party sooner rather than later. It's only noon."

"Don't think I haven't had the same idea." They headed toward the north park. Marsh was glad. It had the best mountain view and the most shade.

"Wonder how much longer till this heat breaks?"

"Wish I knew. It's getting old." He stepped aside while an elderly couple crossed in front of them to enter Halliday's Insurance.

"Aw, they were sweet," Effie said when they'd passed. "But do you ever feel like we're the youngest folks in town?"

He chuckled. "Now that you mention it—yes. Just wait till the wedding. We'll be the youngest at the altar by forty years."

"It's funny, but also kind of sad. Wish Wallace and Mabel had met sooner, but who knows? Maybe having each other will give both of them such a health boost that they'll live extra years."

"Hope so."

They waited for five cars and a truck hauling a cattle trailer to pass before crossing the street to the park.

They meandered down a winding blacktop path until reaching an aspen-filled glade. It was too hot for the usually alpine trees, and the leaves drooped.

"Those trees look how I feel."

Effie laughed, then sat on a bench near a man-made gurgling stream. Her pale blue sundress matched her eyes, and Marsh fought an irrational urge to tug the band barely holding her long hair in place.

"Now that—"

"What do you—"

After both tried speaking at once, they shared a smile.

"Ladies first," Marsh said.

"All right…" She ducked her gaze and now held her hands tightly clasped. "I'm not even sure where to start. I guess I was going to say that now that I've got you alone, I've got an odd question for you—and if you're not interested or it feels forced, I completely understand."

"That's the most intriguing thing I've heard in a while. What's up?" *Is she asking me on a date? Why else would she need me alone?* She'd never given any indication that she was even attracted. *But if she is?* He wasn't sure how he'd feel. Since his divorce, women had been the last thing on his mind.

"Well…" Beneath her freckles, her cheeks turned an appealing pink.

Shit. Should he man up and ask her out? "Effie, if you want to go on a—"

"Marsh, I need you to—"

They cut each other off again, but this time it was good, because Marsh welcomed the comic relief. With luck, she'd aborted her mission and realized she wouldn't want to spend any more time than necessary with a head case like him.

She forced a breath, then began again. "The other afternoon at the house, when you made Remington forget his missing eyeball—" she grimaced "—you had such a great way of calming him without babying him like I always seem to do. At the time, it might not have seemed like much, but your help meant a lot to me."

"It was no big deal. You forget I used to be a dad. I know how kooky kids sometimes get."

"Oh, I know—which is why I feel bad even asking you this, but would you consider spending an hour or two a week with my boys? I'd gladly do a favor for you in return. Clean or cook—whatever. It's just that the older they get, the more I feel like they need a strong male influence, and unfortunately, their dad took himself out of the picture."

She didn't want him to spend time with her, but with her kids?

Wow, Marsh, you're even further off your game than you thought.

"I know it's a lot to ask, but last night, the boys tried to mop the baby, and—"

"Hold up—they what?"

"Long story." Her adorably toothy grin made him a little sad she hadn't wanted that date. "Honestly, I'm not even sure what I'd need you to do. I'm just struggling with discipline—mostly with Colt—and wondering if I devise a way to nip trouble now, it won't get worse once he's older."

"Makes sense." What didn't was the way Marsh realized he'd leaned closer while she'd been talking, rapt with interest over anything she had to say. The corners of her lips had the cutest crinkle, and at that moment, he would have agreed to anything to spend more time watching her talk, which was confusing as hell.

"Then you'll do it?"

"It would be a privilege."

She exhaled. "I wasn't sure how you'd take it. I thought you might think I'm a kook. Plus, I worried if being around Colt and Remington might bother you since, well, you know…"

"What happened with my son?" His jaw hardened, and he nodded. "The funny thing is, your guys are so much older than he was that it's somehow different. With your daughter, I remember those baby stages, but Colt and Remington are a couple of characters who make me happy—not sad."

"Good. Then we have a deal?" She held out her hand for him to shake.

"Hold up—not so fast." He couldn't resist teasing her. "You mentioned that we'd be exchanging services. What do I get?"

"Oh—of course." She reddened again, and he liked the rev it brought to his pulse. "Well, I can clean, exercise your horses, cook—"

"Yahtzee. Me and Wallace live on TV dinners and pork 'n' beans. How about a couple times a week, you bring over your crew and I'll take them out riding, teach them about horses and cattle, and hopefully sneak in a few life lessons? Meanwhile, you and Cass can be inside, whipping up a meat loaf or spaghetti—oh, and pie. Lord, I've missed pie."

"Deal." They shook on it. "I take it your wife was a great cook?"

"Yeah…" He hadn't thought anything positive about Leah in ages. Hard to believe they'd once been in love. Where had it gone? All the emotion he'd once felt for her?

"What's wrong? You look sad. If you're having second thoughts, we can—"

"I'm good. I was thinking about my ex. You ever wonder how a marriage that starts out promising turns out to be a dud? Like, I get losing our son was rough on us both, but how did we also lose each other?" Marsh hadn't meant to admit any of that out loud, but something about Effie gave safety to his confession.

She cupped her hand over his, filling him with warmth he wasn't sure he deserved but certainly appreciated. Once again, Effie had slipped into angel mode. She seemed to constantly be looking out for others, but when did she focus on herself?

He flipped her hand, clasping it, ignoring bolts of awareness of her not as a friend, but as a desirable woman. He glanced up to find her eyes wide and her pupils dilated. Her lips had been pressed, but now she held them barely parted. Effie Washington wasn't just pretty, but beautiful.

"There you two are." Wallace approached.

Marsh released Effie's hand as if they'd been playing hot potato.

"My lady's all in a dither about the dessert course. She thinks the wedding cake is enough, but hell, I say let's have cake, pie and one of those fancy chocolate fountains."

Marsh shared a look with Effie, and the two of them laughed.

"What's funny about any of that?" Wallace asked.

"Nothing at all." Effie rose, then shocked Marsh by reaching out her hand to help him from the bench. The gesture was sweet. As soon as he was standing, she let him go. But a pang told him he didn't want her to.

Another pang told him he had to. He couldn't take another loss, and considering how much he'd grown to enjoy Effie's company, once they inevitably parted ways, no good could come. She'd eventually meet the kind of stand-up rock who could be a great second dad to her brood and adoring husband to her. She deserved all of that and more.

Hell, if his past hadn't been such a disaster, he might have even tossed his hat into her proverbial ring, but his days for romance were long gone. If he were smart, he wouldn't have agreed to spend time with her boys, but now that he'd already given his word, he intended to stick by it.

Why? Not only was it the right thing to do, but he couldn't bear being the reason Effie lost her smile.

Chapter Seven

That night, after three exhausting attempts to get the boys to bed, Effie finally retired to the living room to fold laundry. Mabel was poring through a stack of bridal magazines, searching for the perfect dress.

It had rained all afternoon, and for once, the temperature was actually pleasant.

"What did you and Marsh talk about? You two were gone so long that you missed desserts."

"Sorry. We actually agreed on a trade. Each week, in exchange for a few meals, he's going to spend time with the boys."

"Hallelujah. That Colt is a rascal. While you were giving Cassidy her bath, I caught him outside, pouring my strawberry jam on an anthill to see what would happen."

Effie groaned. "Hope they weren't fire ants?"

"If they had been, don't you think you'd have heard about it by now?"

"True…" Effie tossed another tiny T-shirt onto Remington's pile.

"Wallace told me he caught you and his grandson holding hands. Should we plan for a double wedding?"

"No." Cheeks burning, Effie folded faster. "Marsh and I are friends—that's all." Granted, he was stupid handsome, rocked the heck out of his cowboy hat and

Wranglers, and was a serious sweetheart to her boys, but that's where the extent of her appreciation for him ended. One day she might think about dating, but not now. Not when her children needed to be her top priority and her soul still felt fragile from having her own personal bull rider stomp all over it.

A WEEK LATER on a Wednesday, after the twins had gotten home from school, Marsh had no sooner accepted delivery of the purchase he probably shouldn't have made but couldn't resist when she pulled up in her ragtag minivan.

Summer had returned with a vengeance, and he tugged his hat's brim lower to shade his eyes from the glare.

Looked as though the whole gang had come, as not only did the boys shoot like twin rockets from the vehicle, but Effie helped Mabel emerge, and then walked around the side for Cassidy.

While the twins were occupied with one of Wallace's corny quarter-behind-their-ears tricks, Marsh sauntered up behind Effie. "Need help?"

"Oh, hey. As a matter of fact, I could use a spare hand. The car seat buckle's stuck."

"Let me take a look." Marsh had expected Effie to move, but she didn't. Which presented a problem. Her proximity put him on high alert—for what, he wasn't sure. All he knew was that being close enough to smell roses in her hair momentarily made him freeze. He waited for the unwelcome awareness of her curves brushing against his to pass, but when it only grew stronger, he focused on finishing the task at hand.

A few hard tugs netted a freed baby, which sent him backing to a safe distance.

"Thanks." Her smile had its usual effect—making him

want to see more, to deserve more, to be the one person in her world who produced it the most.

"No problem."

"Hope you like spaghetti—Mabel said it's Wallace's favorite." She took the infant from her seat.

"Love it, but I thought this was my trade," he teased. "Shouldn't you be fixing my favorite?" Once Cassidy rode on Effie's hip while tugging a chunk of her mama's hair, Marsh followed the pair to the van's hatchback for grocery-carrying detail.

"Sorry. I should have asked you first."

"I'm messing with you. Trust me, I'll eat anything. One time in Argentina—"

"What was the US Navy doing in Argentina?"

"Nothing worth talking about. Let's just say one time when my team and I were out on a mission, the target we'd been following led us miles from our base camp. By the time we got back, even though we'd strung up our food supplies, freaking monkeys had eaten it all. With a good ten days left in the mission, we ate rats and slugs. So when I tell you I'll eat anything, I mean it."

"Good to know." Her over-the-shoulder grin played havoc with his gut. Damn, she was a beauty. Then there was her cutie-pie daughter blowing raspberries at him on her way into the house. As a pair, the two of them were lethal to his resolve to steer clear of females.

Judging by the happy shrieks coming from the side yard, Wallace had shown the twins his old tire swing.

"What do you have planned for the boys?" Effie asked.

"With your permission, we're going riding." They'd reached the house, and since she had a free hand, she opened the front door for him to pass through. He tried not brushing against her, but with his hands full, failed. When his shoulder collided with a portion of her anatomy that was far too full and yielding to have been anything other than her breast, he lurched back as if encountering a second rattler. "Sorry."

"It's okay." Judging by her flushed expression, the moment had been equally awkward.

Eager to get his mind back to her twin boys rather than twin *assets*, Marsh said, "I got a great deal on a pair of ponies from a neighbor. Thought your guys might find them easier to ride than our quarter horses."

"That's so sweet, but you didn't have to do that. How much were they? I'll find a way to reimburse you."

"No need." He set the groceries on the kitchen table. "I thought it might be good to teach the boys the responsibility of caring for animals. I know they help with your chickens and stuff, but…" He hadn't meant to come off like a parenting pro. "Not that you aren't already doing a great job of teaching them everything, but you know what I mean."

"Sure." With the baby still on her hip, she'd started unloading. "I get it. And trust me, if I thought I was a perfect parent, I wouldn't have asked for your help. It doesn't say much for my marriage that the thing I most miss about being a couple is having Moody's help with the kids."

"That's understandable. Kids create quite a bond." In his case, after Tucker's passing, he and Leah had both realized their son had been the only part of each other's lives that they shared. They'd tried counseling, but when Marsh kept missing sessions due to work, she'd called quits on their marriage, and honestly? He'd been relieved. Not seeing Leah meant not having to witness the blame written all over her face for their perfect little boy dying on Marsh's watch.

"I used to think so, but my ex has had no problem

moving on. I think part of my discipline problem has been the fact that the twins somehow blame me for their father being gone."

"You think so?" He folded her cloth shopping bags.

"I guess that assumption isn't an absolute, but it would make sense."

"Maybe? But on the flip side—"

"Mom! Mom!" The back door practically exploded open and twin boy power rocketed through. "Guess what?"

Cassidy had been startled by the sudden noise, and looked huffy and on the verge of tears.

"What? And please use inside voices. Remember this isn't our home." Effie jiggled her daughter and delivered playful, sloppy kisses to her cheek to coax back her smile.

Marsh parked against the counter, comfortable watching from the sidelines.

"Sorry," Remington said. Last time they'd been together, Marsh noted a cowlick on the right side of his head that his brother didn't have.

"Mom!" Undaunted, Colt was louder than ever. "They have two ponies! And a swing! And we get to ride everything!"

"That's awesome. Marsh is pretty great, huh?"

"Yeah! Thanks!" When both boys ambushed him in a hug, Marsh was lost. He'd forgotten how easily affection was given at a young age. Everyone's your friend, and reality rarely extended beyond your immediate family, school and current best friend.

For Marsh, on the other hand, reality was a pint-size grave back in Virginia. But here, now, in this moment, he looked forward to an afternoon of showing Effie's little cowboys their way around a barn and then sitting down to a home-cooked meal. Part of him would always harbor guilt and shame and regret for feeling any happiness, but he wasn't opposed to helping others find theirs.

TWO HOURS LATER—after a saddling lesson, then giving each boy a safety helmet for a ride to one of his favorite natural springs—Marsh showed the boys a fun way to cool down their ponies and his horse with supersize sponges and buckets of water he'd left out so they would give good evaporation cooling but not be too cold.

Of course, the boys ended up getting more water on themselves than the ponies, but that was all right. For their first day, they'd done great.

"Guys, come on in the barn, and let's put up your saddles and grab a few brushes."

"Okay," Remington said.

"No! I'm hot and wanna play in the water!" Colt jumped into the trough, in the process splashing out half the water Marsh had earlier added.

"Colt," Marsh said, "get out."

"No! You're not my dad and I don't have to!" He smacked his hands atop the water, not only wasting precious H_2O, but spooking the ponies and Marsh's horse.

Marsh had wondered how long Colt's good behavior would last, and actually, it had been a lot longer than he'd expected. But now he had quite a situation on his hands that he wasn't sure how to handle.

Following gut instinct, while Remington watched, Marsh strode to the trough and planted his hands beneath Colt's scrawny arms, hefting him kicking and screaming out of the water.

"No! Stop! I wanna swim! I'm gonna tell my dad you're a bad person, and he's gonna punch you right in your ugly nose!"

Wow. That escalated quickly.

"Okay, first," Marsh said after setting the dripping kid on a split-log bench in the corral's far end, "you're going to apologize to your brother, me, then the ponies and my horse for acting a fool."

"No, I'm not! I hate you!" Colt tried getting up, but Marsh gently pushed him back down.

"Fair enough. But second, if you want to be a real cowboy, you need to learn respect—not just for your fellow cowboys, but the animals you depend on to help you do your work. Do you remember that day I got snake bit, and your mama found me on my horse?"

"Yeah…" He touched his chin to his chest.

"What do you think would have happened if my pal Whiskey hadn't carried me to your house?"

"You could've been dead!" Remington offered.

"True. But since I'm not, don't you think I'm awfully lucky I have such a smart horse? And don't you think because he's so good to me, I should be good to him?"

"I love my pony," Colt said. "But I *hate* you!"

"I don't care." Only Marsh did. It broke his heart to see Colt's outward demonstration of what had to be an awful lot of pent-up pain. But that was okay. He had a tough skin and wasn't going anywhere. Effie had done the right thing in asking him to help, and he wouldn't let her or her boys down. "Now, once you've cooled off, I'm going to need you to make those apologies, then refill the water trough, so the horses and ponies have plenty of clean water."

"No!"

Remington said, "Colt, you're gonna be in big trouble." *"Noooooooooo!"*

Marsh joined the stubborn little mule on the bench, leaned back against the barn wall and stretched out his legs, crossing them at the ankles. "Rem, do me a favor and please brush your pony. Remember how I showed you?"

"Uh-huh!" He ran for the tack room.

"You guys about done?" Effie strolled up with Cassidy all smiles on her hip. "Supper's ready whenever you are."

"I'm starving!" Colt leaped up, but Marsh gave him a gentle nudge right back down.

"Actually, we've got a bit of business to take care of out here. Remington's going to brush his pony, then he'll be right in. Colt's got a few more things to do, but I'm sure none of it will take too long, right, bud?"

"I hate you, and I'm not doing nothing!" He struggled to get up again, but Marsh held his arm against Colt's chest just firm enough to anchor the wriggling boy to the bench.

"Colt," Effie warned in a low tone. "What did you do?"

"Nothing! He's a monster man and I hate him!"

"Mommy!" Remington ran to the corral fence to meet his mom. He held the brush. "Colt's been bad, but I was good!"

"Thank you, sweetie." Through the wide fence slats, she smoothed his hair. "How about you finish up the chores Mr. Marsh has for you, then come inside to wash up."

"Okay!"

Marsh couldn't get over the difference in the two boys. For all of their exterior similarities, on the inside, they couldn't be more unique.

Colt announced with crossed arms and a scowl, "I'm not doing nothing!"

"You're not doing *anything*," his mother corrected, "and as long as Marsh has been kind enough to let you ride his ponies, you have to follow his rules."

"No, no, *no!*" Colt added kicks to his shouting, startling the ponies and his baby sister.

Remington dashed off to soothe both ponies.

Marsh held his arm firm.

He and Effie shared a look.

First and foremost, Colt was her son, and if she didn't agree with his way of handling the situation, all she had to do was speak up and Colt would be off house arrest. When she gave him a barely perceptible nod, then mouthed *thank you*, he took that as his sign to proceed with his tough love.

"Rem, hon," she called, "as soon as you're done, come inside. I made your favorite garlic toast."

"Yum! Thanks, Mom!"

"No fair!" Colt hollered. "That's *my* favorite!"

"You're welcome, Rem. Colt, sweetie, hurry before supper gets cold."

Colt growled and thrashed, but Marsh held firm. He'd broken horses and entire terrorist cells. A six-year-old kid he could handle—not that Colt needed breaking, but Marsh guessed he needed reassurance someone in his life cared enough about him to ensure he toed the line. Of course, his mother did, but for whatever reason, that wasn't enough.

Effie waved, then coaxed Cassidy, "Wave goodbye to your brothers and Mr. Marsh."

The infant waved her chubby arm and hand, drooling through a grin.

The sight of mother and child tightened Marsh's chest. On autopilot, he returned the little angel's wave, but he felt lost inside. How many times had Leah coached Tucker into the same action? Each time Marsh had damn near popped with pride over his clever son. Finding joy in another child's skills made him feel almost traitorous to his son's memory. Then there was what he felt for Effie. Part appreciation for the unexpected richness she and her children had unwittingly brought to his life. Part affection for the role she'd played in nursing him back to health after his bite. Part attraction for the woman in her that made him crave more than chaste brushes against her curves or merely holding her hand.

He wanted to push aside her ponytail and nuzzle her neck. Would she taste sweat salty? He forced the thought from his mind. This was neither the time nor place—not that there would ever be a right occasion for putting the moves on a woman who had enough of her own problems and sure as hell didn't need to be saddled with his.

Effie and Cassidy went inside, and once Marsh told Remington he'd done a good job with brushing both ponies, he scampered into the house, as well.

An hour passed, and though Marsh couldn't wait to taste Effie's meal, there was no way he was budging. As much as he was testing Colt, the boy was also testing him.

Marsh felt bad for not brushing Whiskey, but right after his sponge bath, he'd taken a dust bath, then trotted off for a visit with his favorite mare.

The sun was setting, and the night's first coyote howled.

Colt said, "If that coyote eats me, my mom's gonna be *real* mad at you."

"Thanks for the warning."

"You don't care if I get ate?"

"Oh—I'd care a lot if you were eaten. I don't want your mom mad."

"Then you better let me go."

"Are you ready to do what I asked without pitching a fit?"

The quiet night was parted by coyote yips.

"Maybe?" Colt's gaze darted toward the west pasture.

"Good. Since your brother already took care of your pony, I'll need you to fill the trough and apologize to me and your brother and both ponies, and also to your mom and little sister."

"What'd I do to them?" He kicked the ground with the toe of his dusty boot.

"Scared her with all your noise."

"Those stupid coyotes scare me all the time, and they don't say sorry."

"Good point, but since they can't talk and you can, I expect better from you."

"Sorry. But I still hate you."

"Fair enough."

"Sorry, ponies. I love you."

"As long as you're good to them, I'm pretty sure they'll love you, too."

"I don't know how to put in the water."

Marsh rose. "I'll be happy to show you."

Once the trough was filled, Marsh had Colt help get the ponies into their shared stall for the night, and then they walked to the house. "Before eating, don't forget to apologize to your brother, mom and sister, okay?"

"I will! You don't *hafta* remind me."

Marsh contemplated scolding him again for this latest outburst but figured the kid had had enough for one day.

They walked in on a happy family setting. Wallace was recounting one of his old oil-field stories—a G-rated one—and Mabel hung on his every word. Effie and Remington sat with their heads together over a math workbook, and Cassidy had more finely chopped spaghetti on her face than in her tummy.

For a moment, even though Colt charged ahead, Marsh clung to the living room's shadows. He used to be part of a vibrant family. His parents and cousins and aunts and uncles back east were always having Leah, Tucker and him over for meals. Back on base, his SEAL team formed another close-knit unit. Now he felt like a stranger looking in. Sure, he and his grandfather were close, and he would soon be related by marriage to everyone else assembled, but what did any of that really mean? Ever since losing his family, he'd longed for nothing more than to once again feel part of something bigger than himself.

But at what cost?

Sure, he could surrender his heart again—not necessarily to Effie and her crew—but would he survive potentially losing it? Moreover, for allowing his son to die on his watch, did he even deserve the privilege of being loved or loving another child?

Chapter Eight

"Sorry, Mom. Sorry, Cass. Sorry, Rem. Can I eat now?"

Effie glanced up from Remington's math homework to find Colt looking dirt smudged and anything but apologetic, but she supposed this was at least a start.

"Thank you for the apologies, and please wash your hands and face. The bathroom's right down the hall." She pointed him that direction.

Marsh entered the big country kitchen, then washed his hands at the sink.

"How'd you get him to come around?" Effie asked.

"I didn't. Coyotes did."

Wallace chuckled. "Count on a few good howls to put the fear of God in little tykes. Your mama used to love catching fireflies, but the second she heard a yip, she'd run for cover. She is coming to the wedding, right?"

"Last time I spoke to her she was checking if she could get away for that date. Dad, too."

"Good, good. But they'll make it, right? You'll talk to them?"

"I'll see what I can do."

Effie cleared her throat. "Marsh, how about you take a seat, and I'll fix you and Colt plates."

"Sounds good. Thanks." His slow grin flip-flopped her stomach. He'd removed his cowboy hat for their meal, and even though his longish hair was a rummaged-through mess, he was still too handsome for a girl to think straight. Tossing in the fact that he'd actually wrangled an apology from her obstinate son made him all the more attractive.

"Marsh," Mabel said, "I'm not sure if I mentioned it, but you and the groomsmen have a tux fitting at Pearl's Bridal at two, Saturday afternoon. She special orders all of her suits from Denver, so it shouldn't take long to take the measurements."

He pulled out a chair at the table. "It's between the feed store and flea market, right?"

"That's the one. It's pink, so you can't miss it."

"Grandma," Effie said, "what are you doing about your dress? You've got almost everything covered but what you're wearing."

"True." Mabel took a slice of garlic toast from a basket in the table's center. "But does an old woman like me really need anything fancy?"

"Damn straight," Wallace said.

"Gramma, I'll make you a dress," Remington said.

"Aren't you a sweetheart," she said to her great-grandson. "Thank you, darling."

He beamed.

"I've got the boys' bank field trip tomorrow, but we could go dress shopping Friday." Effie set warmed plates in front of Marsh and Colt, who'd returned from the bathroom with still-dripping hands. Effie used a dish towel to dry them.

"Marsh," Wallace asked, "where are you in regard to finding our girls a new ride? Thought I told you to get them a loaded SUV with all the bells and whistles?"

"Wallace—" Effie erased Remington's wrong numbering sequence in his math workbook "—you're a doll to make that kind of offer, but we couldn't accept. Besides, my old minivan works just fine."

He snorted. "*Fine* might be good enough for some folks, but not for me. Once Mabel and I start traveling, neither one of us will sleep a wink knowing you're back here with car worries."

"But it's never given us a lick of trouble."

"For *now...*" he said with a lift of his bushy eyebrows. "But what happens a few months down the road? Everyone knows once winter hits with a vengeance, car batteries are notoriously cranky."

"Listen to him," Mabel said. "For heaven's sake, the man wants to buy you a brand-spanking-new car. Why don't you let him?"

"It's the principle of the thing." As could all too easily become habit, she looked to Marsh for support. "Help me out here. Tell your grandfather not to toss his money around to strangers."

"I could tell him," he said with a wry smile, "but that doesn't mean he'll listen."

"It's settled." Wallace thumped the table hard enough to rattle the mismatched plates, cups and saucers. "Effie, my dear, I understand this week is plumb full up, but next week, Marsh is taking you into Colorado Springs for a new ride. End of story."

The man was offering her a new car. The van had one hundred and eighty thousand miles. What was her problem? Maybe the fact that Moody had been bad about telling her what to do. Or then again, maybe she felt a sentimental connection to that old car. During lean times, she and Moody had practically lived in it, and all three of her kids had been brought home from the hospital in it. In ways, that van was the last of an era to which she wasn't quite ready to say goodbye.

"Slow down there, Gramps." A warm flush filled her at the prospect of Marsh jumping to her defense. "Effie's a grown woman, and if she says she doesn't want a new car, you should respect her wishes."

"Not if they're stupid!"

Mabel gave him the stink eye. "Did you just call my granddaughter stupid?"

The boys turned their heads back and forth as if they were at a tennis match.

Cassidy focused on her cookie dessert.

Rocket, the cat, sat beneath her licking up all that the baby dropped.

"Oh, now look what you've gone and done," Wallace complained with a grumble. "There's no sense in every-one getting all riled up. Mabel, my love, maybe I'm not calling Effie stupid, but slow. I mean, who turns down a brand-new car?"

"That's it." Mabel slammed her napkin to the table. "Boys, find a dishrag to clean up your baby sister, be-cause it's high time for us to go."

"Honey bunch." Wallace left his seat to help her up from hers. "Don't go getting your panties in a wad. Let's talk this out."

"Nothing more to say." She wrenched off her massive ring and pitched it at him. "The wedding's off. Wallace Stokes, I always knew you were a darned fool, and now it's been confirmed. Just because you're a handsome devil doesn't give you the right to tell my sweet granddaugh-ter what to do."

To the twins, she said, "Hustle. And please grab my reusable shopping bags off the counter."

To Effie, she said, "I'll meet you in the van."

"Mabel, wait!" Wallace chased after his ex-fiancée.

Effie caught Marsh's gaze and couldn't help but crack

a smile. "Are those two crazy, or am I the one a few apples shy of a bushel?"

"The two of them are certifiable."

"Wait," Effie teased, "did you just call my grandma crazy?"

"Guilty." Grinning, he held up his hands in surrender. "What's my punishment?"

"A kiss." She covered her mouth with her hands. "Sorry. I can't believe that popped out. Whenever my ex and I used to play fight, the loser owed a kiss. Guess it's been a while since I flirted with anyone—not that I was flirting, or we were. You know what I mean, right? How as couples you get into a routine and then at the oddest times, you feel transported back, like nothing changed—only everything changed." She covered her blazing cheeks with her hands. "Listen to me. I must sound cuckoo for Cocoa Puffs."

"I want Cocoa Puffs," Colt said while swiping a wet dishrag across his sister's sauce-covered hands. "I love cereal!"

"Me, too," Remington said.

Effie had expected Marsh to run from her, but he instead stepped closer and closer until she got the impression he might intend to kiss her. The boys and Cassidy were right there with them, yet for all the bustle and little boy chatter, everything faded but the cowboy of whom she never quite seemed to get her fill. Her pulse galloped, her breathing slowed and her body welcomed whatever he might have to offer, but no way was she emotionally ready. *Right?*

"Effie, I…" He inched toward her, and when their gazes locked, it produced a flutter low in her belly. *OMG*—was he going to kiss her? Did she actually want him to? He now stood mere inches away, close enough for her to imagine every strong inch of him radiating against her soft curves. "I'm…jeez, I'm really sorry about my grandfather's ham-fisted tactics."

"It's okay. I'm not sure why I got so upset over a sweet old guy wanting to give me a car." She forced a smile.

Marsh backed away.

But she'd been so certain he'd be doing anything but talking with his sexy mouth that when he didn't kiss her, it took a moment to regain her bearings. What had she been thinking?

Clearly, she wasn't!

Sure, she and Moody had shared affection in front of the boys, but they'd been husband and wife. She and Marsh were—well, for lack of a better word, they were *nothing*. At best, casual friends—not in the least bit romantic. So why was her pulse still racing?

"*Ew!*" Colt had run to the front door with Mabel's bags but now returned to the kitchen making faces. "Grandma and Grandpa Wallace are kissing!"

Effie found herself sharing another look with Marsh and couldn't help but laugh.

"Guess she'll be needing this?" she asked after plucking her grandmother's engagement ring from the kitchen floor.

"Looks that way."

The once again happy couple strolled through the front door.

"The wedding's back on," Mabel said. "And Effie, Wallace has something he'd like to say to you."

Effie raised her eyebrows. *This should be good…*

"Angel, you may not have noticed, but it's been a while since I was around ladies, and I forget that I can't just bark orders. I genuinely apologize for *ordering* you to get a new car, but please know that from the bottom of my heart, I want you and your precious cargo to be safe and secure. I've got more money than I know what to do with, and it would make me a happy man to see all that cash do some good before I'm gone."

Wallace's from-the-heart speech welled tears in Effie's eyes. Compelled to hug him, she did just that. "In that case, thank you, and I accept."

"Perfect." He clapped his hands. "Maybe we can all go on Saturday and make a day of it? Kill two birds with one stone by grabbing a car and a wedding dress."

"I don't wanna kill a bird!" Remington started crying.

Which made Cassidy cry.

Which made Effie say, "All right, I think it's past some folks' bedtimes, and a certain little lady still needs a bath." She kissed Cassidy's sticky cheek.

After a round of goodbyes, by the porch light's glow and crickets' chirps, Marsh and Wallace helped carry bags and sleepy boys to the van, then got everyone buckled in.

Effie was behind the wheel with the motor running when Marsh approached the window.

She lowered it. "What's up?"

"I wanted to tell you to drive careful. And thanks again for the laughs. It felt good."

"I know, right?" There went her pulse again. He'd pressed his open palms against the door frame, which raised his T-shirt enough to bare a strip of skin and his wholly masculine happy trail. Mouth dry, she forced her gaze to his eyes, but that didn't do much to help stop the tingly awareness that lately, more often than not, took hold whenever he was around.

"Anyway, good night, Effie."

"'Night." The sound of her name pronounced nice and slow with his hint of a Southern twang produced all manner of havoc in her belly. If she hadn't been crammed into an old minivan that smelled like Cheerios with her grandmother and a pack of kids, would he have kissed her?

Forcing her focus on the drive home rather than the carnal drives that kept cropping up, once Marsh backed away, then waved, she smiled before aiming the van for home.

"Is it just me?" Mabel fastened her seat belt. "Or is that boy sweet on you?"

"Grandma, *really*?" Effie cast a sideways glare. How did Mabel know what she'd been thinking? Was it that obvious that she harbored a secret anti-crush on their neighbor?

"Would that be so bad? He's handsome and all alone. You're pretty as a picture and far from alone. Looks to me like a match made in heaven."

"Looks to me like you may have had a little too much of Wallace's homemade wine. Oh—and here…" She fished Mabel's ring from her sundress pocket. "You forgot it on your fiancé's kitchen floor."

"Oops." Mabel giggled. "That man does have a way of chapping my hide. But he also makes my heart sing."

"I'm glad. It's nice seeing you happy."

"You know what would really make me smile?"

"What?"

"Seeing you just as happy. Should we shoot for that double wedding?"

Effie laughed, then glanced at Mabel. In the dash light's glow, she was shocked to find her serious. "You're not joking?"

"Hon, I don't mean to get in your business, but when's the last time you were good and thoroughly kissed? Trust me, a little nooky does a body good…" Mabel might have winked, but Effie rammed on the gas pedal.

Chapter Nine

The day of the first grade bank field trip, Effie put extra effort into packing the boys' lunches. After the behind-the-scenes bank tour, the plan was to walk the children to the city park playground where they'd eat and work off excess energy before heading back to school.

She was midway through making her third ham sandwich when Colt asked, "Mom, in case there's robbers, I'm gonna bring my gun, okay?"

"Sweetie, I appreciate that you want to help keep everyone safe, but I don't think that's a good idea."

"Can I at least wear my cowboy hat and gun holster?" His pout showed that to his way of thinking, her verdict was far from acceptable.

"Sweetie…" She sighed. How had she gotten lucky enough to have the most precocious first grader on the planet? "How about if you just wear one of your best superhero T-shirts? That way, if there's any trouble, you'll be ready to call Batman or Superman or Hulk—whoever you think would be best for the job."

"I guess that would work. But it's not the same."

"I know." She kissed the crown of his head. "But banks are pretty serious places. Promise you'll be on your very best behavior? No fooling around?"

When she hugged him, he squirmed free.

Typical of the men in her life.

Her mind's eye flashed to Marsh. How long before he was gone? He couldn't be on leave from the Navy forever. Eventually, they'd expect him back. Already, she felt an odd kinship with him—all the more so since their chat in the park. She'd been touched when he opened up to her about his failed marriage.

As much as her own failed marriage hurt, she found an odd comfort in knowing she wasn't the only one who had questions about how loves that had started out good and pure could turn wrong on a dime. In Marsh's case, the loss of a son had been an understandable stress on his marriage, but in her case, she'd always wondered what she'd done wrong. If she'd supported Moody's bull riding instead of nagging him about settling down to start a cozy home, would they still be together?

After a quick thanks and hug to Mabel for watching Cassidy, Effie loaded the boys and was off. She used the thirty-minute drive to town to go over basic rules and manners. No running inside. Please and thank you. Use inside voices. Etc., etc.

She'd been over each item a zillion times, but a bank was hardly the place for one of the boys to forget.

By the time Effie found a parking space in the school's undersized lot, then got both boys to class, they were seconds from being tardy. She was out of breath when she made it to the back of the room to join the five other moms going on the outing.

"Hey, you." Scotty's mom, Patricia, greeted Effie with a hug. "I was worried you had a crisis crop up."

"No." Effie set her purse on the bookshelf lining the classroom's rear wall. "It's just tough getting my rowdy crew out of the house. Fingers crossed we have no surprises."

"Amen to that."

The teacher took roll and the children stood for the Pledge of Allegiance.

Hearing so many voices united in patriotism tightened Effie's throat. It made her think of Marsh's service to their country, and what he must have been like when he was on active duty. She pictured him as a good soldier. Strong, yet compassionate.

When her mind's eye got around to picturing him in uniform, she blushed. The man was already too handsome. Toss Navy dress whites on him, and the poor ladies wouldn't stand a chance.

The notion of him having his pick from a bevy of Virginia Beach beauties didn't set well. Not that she was in the position to stake a claim on him, but for some unfathomable reason, she didn't want anyone else to, either.

What did she want? She thought of their shared laughs in his grandfather's kitchen and the way when he'd leaned against her car, if they hadn't had an audience, she might have been sorely tempted to kiss him. But what good would that have done other than making her all the more confused? What man in his right mind would want anything to do with a single mom with three kids? After the wedding, he'd no doubt see her boys, but not her.

Which made her sad.

But that was the way it had to be.

"Effie? Everything okay?" Patricia touched her arm. "We're passing the volunteer sign-up sheet for the school's Thanksgiving dinner, and you seemed a million miles away."

"Sorry. I don't think we've talked since my grandmother got engaged. The wedding is the third week in October, and the planning is making me nuts."

"Wait—we're talking about sweet Mabel?"

"Yep." Effie grinned, glad for the distraction from Marsh. "Hard to believe, right?"

"Not at all. She's a firecracker." Patricia nudged Effie's shoulder. "Now, we need to work on finding you a man. Roy has a super-cute single friend in his office, and we were actually just talking about fixing you two up. Want to double-date?"

"Oh—I couldn't." The mere thought of a formal date had Effie fishing through her purse for antacids.

"Of course, you could. Nothing fancy. Just dinner with friends. I'm setting it up fast—before you have a chance to say no."

"Thought I just did? Say no?"

Patricia laughed. "I didn't hear you."

Thankfully, the teacher, Mrs. Logan, broke up the conversation with instructions and a last-minute flurry of gathering stray permission slips before lining up the kids.

The day was beautiful with a hint of a nip in the air to give hope that cooler fall temps would soon come.

While paused at a street crossing, Effie tipped her head back to drink in the sun. It was the kind of day so beautiful that nothing could dare go wrong. Now that Patricia had abandoned talk of a double date in favor of chatting with another mom about a newly forming peewee basketball league, Effie was apparently off the proverbial hook.

Someday, once the kids were old enough to spend a few hours on their own, she might welcome dating. But for now, most days she didn't just have her hands full, but hog-tied with caring for Cassidy and the twins.

At this time of the morning, the bank wasn't busy, and the manager took the children into a back room. After they'd all assumed their crisscross-applesauce positions on the carpeted floor, he delivered an entertaining history lesson about famous bank robbers who once prowled the Old West.

Usually fidgety Colt hung on the man's every word, as did Remington.

Effie beamed with pride. She'd been silly to worry. Colt might act out with her and even Marsh, but at least on an important day like this, he'd remembered his manners.

The manager finished his stories, then showed the children the safety deposit boxes and gave them a peek inside the main vault.

They were getting a last look behind the tellers' cages when Colt took not one of the plastic pistols his father had gifted him, but two, from his backpack, ran up to a teller and shouted, "*Bang! Bang!* Give me all your money or you're dead!"

"Colt, no!" Beyond mortified, Effie shot into action, but not before her little outlaw snatched a wad of hundreds the startled woman had been counting, then ran out the front door.

Effie chased after her son.

The bank manager and security guard chased after them both.

"Colt, stop! *Stop!*"

"*Bang! Bang!* I'm Jesse James!" Hundred-dollar bills floated behind him.

Out of breath and horrified by the morning's turn of events, when Effie couldn't run farther, she paused to let the two men pass her.

By the time the security guard caught up with Colt, sirens could be heard.

While the bank manager plucked hundreds of dollars from neighboring lawns, Colt struggled with the security guard.

"Leave me alone! I'm Jesse James!"

Effie found her second wind and ran in her son's direction.

"In all my days—" the security guard held firm to Colt's shoulders "—I've never seen anything quite like this."

"I'm so sorry," Effie said. "Colt, what's wrong with you? I told you to leave your guns at home!"

"It's okay, Mom. We're rich!" He flapped his stack of hundreds.

Effie had never despised her ex more—or herself. How had Colt gotten so out of control that he thought this kind of behavior was okay?

Once the police realized their bank robber was shorter than a broomstick, the sirens and lights went off, and Effie caught a few of the guys chuckling.

But to the irate bank manager, this was no laughing matter.

While Effie held back to give the police an official report—they actually asked if she'd put Colt up to his shenanigans—Patricia was kind enough to take Remington to the park with the other children. She said if Effie wasn't back to school in time to pick him up, she would ensure he got on the school bus.

Mrs. Logan suggested it would be best for Colt to not return to school that afternoon, but that she would make an appointment for Effie and him to speak with the principal first thing in the morning.

When a policeman told her and Colt to get in the back of his car for a trip to the station, Effie's heart felt dangerously close to pounding out of her chest.

"Sorry, Mommy," Colt said from beside her.

Sorry? The apology didn't quite cover all that had

transpired. Still, Effie loved her son, and when silent tears streamed down his cheeks, she pulled him into a hug.

"What were you thinking?"

"I just wanted to play cops and robbers. And when that old guy was talking about Jesse James, I wanted to be cool like him, too."

"But, honey, it's not *cool* to rob banks or anything else. Most of those Wild West bank robbers got shot or went to jail. I love you and want a way better life for you."

"Am I going to jail?"

"Honestly, sweetie—" fear knotted her stomach "—I don't know."

Chapter Ten

After sleeping too late, that afternoon, Marsh rode Whiskey out to check his grandfather's livestock.

Wallace had fifty-three head of buffalo. They were ornery and pretty much did what they wanted, but the old coot seemed to love them, so Marsh put up with their cantankerous ways. Honestly, they were more like pets to his grandfather than a means for profit. As far as Marsh knew, Wallace hadn't sold a single one, and his herd started years earlier with twenty.

The day hadn't gotten as warm as expected, and the air smelled loamy and clean. Blue sky rose clear to heaven and for once made him smile when he thought of his boy.

Lord, he missed him.

Wonder what Tucker would think of the twins?

Had he still been alive, he would be older than them. The notion raised a swell of pain that Marsh tamped down by squeezing his eyes shut tight, then opening them to drown in the sky's healing infinity.

He forced deep breaths, focusing on the task at hand of counting the herd and making sure they all looked healthy.

Finished, he took his time getting back to the house.

Rather than dwelling on the son he no longer had, he focused on Effie and her twins, and the way if both of their lives had been less complicated, he might have acted on urges to kiss her. She was pretty and wholesome and uncomplicated in a world that seemed to grow increasingly more tangled. Being with her brought a curious calm, but at the same time, the sort of anticipation he remembered feeling as a kid right before Halloween or Christmas, only in an adult version.

Before he'd met her and her brood, his days had been an endless succession of marathon rides and even longer lonely nights. Now he looked forward to planning activities for her boys. It lightened his spirit to find himself in the position of being able to—in some small way—lighten her load.

He didn't know her ex, but Marsh found himself hating him. What kind of man left a woman who'd had three of his kids? It was unconscionable.

Marsh had ridden within a quarter mile of the barn when his cell vibrated. Out here, service was sketchy. Since his run-in with the rattler, he carried his phone with him more because his grandfather had asked him to than out of any belief that it might one day save his life.

Expecting to have to perform a wedding errand, he took the electronic nuisance from the back pocket of his Wranglers, only to find it hadn't been Wallace calling, but the Maysville Police Department.

Concerned, he reined Whiskey to a stop, afraid that just as they'd moseyed into cell range, they could mosey right back out.

The caller had been Effie. She'd left a voice mail. "Marsh—I'm so sorry to bother you, but I've run into a situation with Colt. I honestly don't know what to do and can't trouble Mabel with this. Since you're busy, I'm sorry. I'll figure something out."

Her tone sounded almost frantic.

He called back, but the call went straight to departmental voice mail.

Stomach clenched with dread for fear her son might have been hurt, Marsh worked Whiskey from a dead stop to a gallop.

"Sorry, bud. Duty calls."

As fast as possible between calls to the station, Marsh brushed Whiskey and made sure he'd cooled and rehydrated in the barn's shade before letting him join his friends in the pasture nearest the house.

Finished, he searched out his grandfather and found him changing his truck's oil in the outbuilding that doubled as a garage.

"Mind handing me that wrench?" Wallace asked from beneath the red Ford.

Marsh did, then hiked himself up to sit on a workbench. "Have you heard from Mabel today?"

"A while back. She said Effie needed your cell number. She's babysitting Effie's youngest all day while the boys take their field trip."

I surmised all that. What Marsh needed to know without alerting Mabel was what had happened on that field trip. Were Effie and the twins in an accident?

"Need anything else?" Marsh asked before heading outside to try reaching her again.

"I'm good. Just about done." The stubborn old man had more money than he knew what to do with but refused to let anyone else change his oil.

On edge and not sure what to do with himself, Marsh reached the station's voice mail once more, then scooped manure from the ponies' stall. He'd let them out to the pasture when he'd first come outside, and they seemed to be getting along fine.

When his cell rang, the chirpy tone damn near made

him jump out of his skin. He glanced at the caller ID—Maysville Police Department.

"Effie?" he answered. "What happened? Are you and the boys okay?"

She broke down.

"Where are you? I'm coming."

"O-outside the police station."

"What? Why?"

"I-it's too long to get into over the phone. But we're okay—at least, we will be." She sniffed.

"Stay put. I'll be right there."

Marsh ran to the house for his keys and wallet, shouted to Wallace that he was headed to town, then hopped in his truck, taking off with enough force to plume dust far behind him.

The trek to blacktop was a bone rattler with his pulse knocking damn near as much as his tires.

What the hell had happened? How had Effie gone from chaperoning a class field trip to crying at the police station?

He made the normally thirty-minute trip in twenty, slowing only upon reaching the quiet facility's lot.

He killed the engine, then spotted Effie rising from a bench.

Halfway between his ride and the entry, they met and he wrapped her in a fierce hug, beyond relieved to see her in one piece. "Where are the boys? Are they okay?"

She nodded against his chest.

Smoothing her long hair, he said, "Tell me what happened."

"The short version is that Colt literally robbed First State Bank."

"Wait—he *what*?" Marsh stepped back. "He was playing, right?"

"Of course, but the offense was apparently so serious that police checked my background to make sure I hadn't put him up to it. The chief is new and seems out to prove himself, so he ordered a battery of psychological tests for Colt—to make sure he's not one of those poor delinquents you hear about on the news. He's stuck in the back room now with a woman from the child welfare agency."

"Lord…" He sighed, then pulled her back into a hug. "I'm so sorry. How's Colt doing?"

"He's rattled, but thank God, answering questions with respect. Dr. Emily Norris assured me in confidence that this would in all likelihood end with her questions, but I'm still scared."

"Of course. Where's Remington?"

She checked her watch. "He should be just about home. I sent him back with the rest of the class and my friend Patricia promised to get him on his bus. All I told Mabel was to watch out for him."

"Good call. No use in both boys being traumatized."

"Marsh, I feel like the worst mom in the world. Why would Colt pull a stunt like that?"

"He's a kid and acted out." He led her back to the bench. "Like you surmised, he's probably pissed about your divorce and the fact that the father he loves abandoned him, but he has no way to show it other than through being an occasional hellion."

"I guess."

"Any chance of calling your ex? You know, to explain how much his son needs him?"

"I did, but he's at a rodeo in Montana. He said he'd try calling Colt later, but I'm not holding my breath. Besides, he thought it was 'cool' that his offspring had already 'fought the law.'"

Marsh cocked his head back and groaned. "Wow. He sounds like a real winner."

"Yep. I can really pick 'em." She laughed through a fresh batch of tears. "Moody always was a rebel. When we first got together, that was part of his attraction. Which was exhilarating. A rush, you know? But once we had the boys, everything changed. I wanted us to create a warm and safe and predictable place for us to call home. He'd agree but always ask for one more rodeo season. Just one more, and then he'd retire and settle down."

"But he never did?"

She shook her head. "The woman he's with now is a pro barrel racer. They have a three-month-old baby girl and take her with them on the road. Not sure what's going to happen once she's old enough for school."

"Thankfully—" Marsh settled his arm around her shoulders and pulled her close enough to kiss the crown of her head "—that's not your problem." He'd meant the gesture to be one of casual comfort for a friend, but affection for her eroded a portion of the protective wall he'd constructed around his emotions. After losing the most precious bonds in his life, Marsh had told himself the best way to never hurt again was to never feel again. But he did. He worried for Effie and Colt. He fought a crazy-ass urge to storm inside the station and rescue Effie's boy.

Effie's boy.

Marsh couldn't lose sight of that fact.

"I'm sorry to bother you with all this." She clung to him, and damn if he didn't automatically tighten his hold, appreciating far more than he'd care to admit—or was even appropriate—the fact that he was once again needed.

"No way could you ever be a bother." He kissed her forehead. "Colt's going to be fine. Hopefully, this turns out to be the sort of brush with the bigger world that scares him straight."

She nodded against him. "When this is over, could you please give us a ride to the school? My van is still there."

"Of course."

"Mrs. Washington." A suit-wearing woman poked her head outside. "We're ready for you."

Marsh stood, helping Effie to her feet. It killed him to notice her slight tremble. "Hey." He turned her to face him. "Everything's going to be fine."

She nodded but didn't look all that sure. "I feel silly for asking, but will you stay with me?"

"Of course." He clasped her hand, giving her fingers a squeeze.

The counselor led them to a brightly lit room at the back of the station, where they found Colt seated in a chair at what Marsh guessed was typically used as an interrogation table. The former parent in him wanted to snatch Colt and take him far from this awful place. On the flip side, he realized this whole situation held the power to serve as a major life lesson.

"Mommy! Mr. Marsh!" The boy leaped from his chair to crush them both in hugs. "I wanna go home!"

"I know, sweetie." Effie looked near tears again. "Hopefully, we're almost done."

"We are," the woman said. "If you don't mind, I'd like to have a female officer watch Colt for a few minutes while we talk. Would that be all right?"

Effie nodded. The transition was smooth once Effie reassured Colt she'd be near.

The police chief joined them.

Marsh rose. Introductions were made, and he labeled himself as a family friend.

"Mrs. Washington, I'm sure it's been a long day for

both you and your son, but I wanted to thank you for your patience. Sadly, the number of crimes committed by children has never been higher, and there are parents out there who would have no moral problem with sending their son or daughter to do an illegal job. I run a tight ship, so please understand that I couldn't take a bank robbery lightly—even one committed by a first grader."

"Of course." Effie sat at the table with her hands clasped.

"Your background check came back clear," the chief droned on, "and of course, your son's did, too. Dr. Norris, I'll turn it over to you for Colt's psychological report."

"Thank you." The woman forced a smile. "Obviously, I didn't have time to do more than a surface-level evaluation of your son, but from what I could tell, Colt is a perfectly normal little boy who harbors resentment toward his father. And some toward you, Mrs. Washington, for your divorce. He even feels partially responsible himself. That said, in my opinion, Colt is too young to understand that what he did today had far more serious repercussions than simply playing a game. But honestly? In my professional opinion, what happened was just that—a game to Colt. He struck me as genuinely sorry for causing a fuss. From here on out, you might take special care to reassure him your divorce had nothing to do with him, and that you and his father love and support him."

Effie nodded. "Thank you, I will."

Beneath the table, she clasped Marsh's hand so tight that it hurt. He knew what she was thinking. Her ex was a selfish bastard, and odds were against him galloping down here on a white steed to save her—not that a strong woman like Effie needed *saving*, but she sure as hell deserved a break.

Finally, the social worker ended her speech and the

chief retrieved Colt and told him he never wanted to see him at the station again.

Finally, mother and son were free to go.

The boy's shoulders slumped and he could hardly keep his eyes open. Acting on pure instinct, Marsh picked him up. He'd halfway expected a protest, but Colt wrapped his slim arms around his neck and rested his head on Marsh's shoulder.

The walk to the truck wasn't long, yet for Marsh, it might as well have taken days. The sensation of once again holding a little boy was heady, forcing him to remind himself this was only a temporary thing.

He gently set Colt on the backseat of his truck's crew cab, then buckled him in.

Behind the wheel with Effie in the passenger seat, Marsh asked, "Need anything at the store before we get your van?"

She shook her head. "I just want to sleep for a week."

"I'll bet." A check in the rearview showed Colt already dozing off. "Sorry your big day turned into a huge freaking nightmare."

"Me, too." She rested her head against the seat back and closed her eyes. "Thanks again for showing up when you did. I owe you—big-time."

"We're good. Consider this payback for when you literally saved my life."

Her sleepy half smile produced an unwelcome yearning in his chest. In that instant, he wanted Effie and her sons and daughter to be *his*. He'd treat them the way a man should—with appreciation and honor. They'd lack for nothing—emotionally or financially. *If* they were his. But they weren't—never would be. Which made him a fool for even thinking about it.

The rest of the short trip to the elementary school,

Marsh focused on driving rather than dwelling on his urge to once again hold Effie's hand. He wouldn't focus on how good it made him feel that Effie had trusted him enough to call in a crisis.

A glance in her direction showed her eyes closed and breathing even. She'd dozed off, too.

If he had any sense of self-preservation, he would have been clinical about the day's events. He wouldn't wonder if he should start paying more attention to Colt if a positive male role model might stop his tantrums and inappropriate stunts. Marsh sure as hell wouldn't think about how lessening Effie's worry would increase the number of times he saw her smile.

At the school, he pulled into the space beside her van but didn't want to let her go. She was in no shape for driving, and after the day he'd had, Colt's broken spirit needed healing, so Marsh left the lot and aimed for the lone road heading out of town.

He'd no doubt have hell to pay once Effie woke to find herself even farther from her van, but that was okay. He'd be more than happy for the excuse to see her again tomorrow when he drove her to pick it up.

The long trip home was quiet.

The last thing Marsh needed was more time for introspection, but somehow, this felt different—better. The sensation of once again contributing rushed through him like a long exhale. After years of feeling useless, he'd again found purpose. But it wasn't supposed to have happened this way.

In her moment of crisis, Effie might have thought she and her brood needed him, but in reality, it was the other way around. He'd been trained to help. That's what he did. He learned of a problem and fixed it. Applying his SEAL values and never-quit attitude to his family had been a natural extension, but then he suddenly had no family and the bottom fell out from under him.

He'd been adrift.

Now, with Effie softly sleeping beside him, his chest swelled with pride for the fact that she felt comfortable and safe enough in his presence to so completely surrender.

But like him, she too had no business depending on anyone. They'd both been badly burned in different ways, and that pain didn't just go away. It forever lurked in dark emotional corners. For all of Marsh's satisfaction in this moment, he couldn't ever fully invest in this woman and her beautiful children, because the pain of possibly losing them would be unfathomable.

Chapter Eleven

Effie woke disoriented.

But then she saw her grandmother's ragtag house on one side and Marsh's handsome profile on the other, and the horrible afternoon flooded back.

"You're awake," he said before turning off the truck's engine. "I'll take you to get your van in the morning. You and Colt looked so wiped, I didn't have the heart to wake you."

"Thanks. It's been quite a day, and I still need to give Mabel the full story. I'm ashamed my son acted that way."

"Don't do that—blame yourself." He looked to ensure Colt was still sleeping. "There were a ton of elements in play. First, I've never heard of a bank allowing such young kids in sensitive areas, and the police were doing their job, but the second they saw the culprit and his toy weapons, they should have realized this was something to laugh about, rather than make a big fuss. Don't get me wrong, I'm not saying what Colt did was good, but half the battle with kids is not putting them in situations where it's all too easy for them to fail. If Colt had been taken on a field trip to the library or a museum, he'd have had a great day."

"I hear you, but when does personal responsibility come into play? He knows better. I get that he thought

he was playing a great game of Old West cops and robbers, but when I told him to stop, he should have. Where
have I gone wrong as a parent that he thinks it was all
right to not only take money, but then run with it? And
keep running until he had to be physically restrained?"
She broke down. "Even my horses are trained better. I
feel worthless as a parent. Lower than low."

"Well, don't." He unfastened his seat belt and pulled
her into another hug. "If you want, I'm here to help and
together, we'll figure this thing out."

"Thank you." Effie melted against him, soaking in
his quiet strength. She could have let him hold her like
this forever. But shouldn't. Experience with her ex taught
her for every second of pleasure and trust and support, it
took days—years—to recover. She couldn't take that risk.

How did she reconcile that fact with the plain and
simple truth that Marsh had been a rock for her and her
son when they'd needed him most?

She closed her eyes, breathing Marsh in. He smelled
incredible. Like the earth and wind and sun-warmed
leather.

"Mom! Mom!" Remington called while running
across the yard to the truck. "Is Colt still in jail?"

Effie bolted from Marsh to compose herself. The last
thing she needed was for her grandmother to catch sight
of a simple hug and read more into it.

"Thanks again," she said to Marsh.

"No problem. Glad I could help." Unbearable sweet-
ness rushed through her when he discreetly took her hand
for a final squeeze. "Seriously, whenever you need me,
don't hesitate to call."

"I appreciate your offer more than you could ever
know." Meeting his intense stare felt akin to looking

too long into the sun, so she lowered her gaze, willing her hammering heart to slow. "Want to stay for dinner?"

"Eff…"

"I'm sorry. You must have things to do." Upon catching hesitation play out across his face, Effie regretted asking. They were barely friends, and already he must think of her as a clingy mess.

"Always."

"I understand." But she didn't. Being in his arms felt like home, but that was a mirage. An unwitting trick of fate she mustn't fall for again—not that Marsh had in any way encouraged her confusion. If anything, he'd been straightforward from the start. She was the one who'd misconstrued his simple kindness for more. She was the one constantly curious about what it might be like to share a kiss. She was the one who'd apparently forgotten the pain of pinning all her hopes and dreams on a man, only to have him leave.

"Let me at least grab Colt for you." Marsh nodded toward the backseat. "He's pretty out of it. I'll carry him straight to bed."

"Yes. Thank you." Wishing he'd change his mind about staying, yet alternately knowing it was best if he didn't, she exited his truck to open the back door. After hugging Remington, she held his hand all the way to the house until he left her to open the screen door for Marsh and Colt.

"Is Colt dead?" he asked after Marsh set his brother on his bed.

"Hush." Mabel clasped Remington's shoulders, drawing him against her. "Come with me to the kitchen, and leave your brother alone."

Effie removed Colt's tennis shoes. Her mothering instincts told her to cover him, but it was far too warm for that, so she made sure the window was open, turned on the ceiling fan, then crept from the room, hyperaware of Marsh's presence behind her.

He closed the door. "His time in the big house must have taken a toll. He's zonked."

"Good." Effie leaned against the nearest wall, finally allowing herself to exhale. More than anything, she longed to step right back into Marsh's strong embrace. She wanted him to hold her and promise everything would be okay. But that was silly. Not only didn't life hand out guarantees, but she'd made it this far on her own, and just like any other crisis, she'd handle this one, too.

What if I don't want to?

Ah, there was the real issue. Late at night, deep in the most secret place in her heart, Effie struggled with the fact that she'd grown weary of facing her every joy and challenge alone. Sure, she had Mabel and her kids, but they were hardly the same as having a true partner in life—the kind of everyday companion she'd once had in her ex. Those early days of their relationship had been heady, painfully similar to the pleasurable tingles she felt whenever she and Marsh shared the same space.

"You do know worrying won't help?" Marsh alternately teased and thrilled her by running his finger along the twin frown lines between her brows. "Colt's going to be fine."

"I know." What would Marsh say if he knew she hadn't been ruminating on her troubles with her son, but him? What kind of mom did that make her?

She covered her face with her hands.

"Now what's the matter?" he asked.

"You wouldn't understand."

"Try me."

After a shake of her head, she couldn't help but grin. She was a basket case. Thank goodness mind reading wasn't one of Marsh's superhuman Navy SEAL skills.

"Arrrgggghh!" Cassidy rolled her walker from the kitchen into the hall fast enough to slam into Marsh's legs.

"Dang, girl." He knelt to honk her ride's horn. "Do you have a license for that thing?"

She cooed and giggled and held up her arms to be picked up.

Of course, Marsh obliged, and for Effie, the sight of her daughter being held in his sturdy embrace made her all the more confused. On the surface, he seemed to be everything her ex wasn't. But that brought no guarantees.

People—just like hearts—changed.

"Marsh, hon!" Mabel called from the kitchen. "Should Remington set a place for you at the supper table?"

Effie held her breath while waiting for his answer.

Had she imagined it, or had he tightened his hold on Cassidy?

"Thank you, ma'am, but I should be getting back. Wallace is expecting me."

"All right. Well, at least let me make the two of you a couple of plates to go."

"Thank you, ma'am," he said in the kitchen.

Effie trailed after him. Was she the reason he wasn't staying? Because she'd hit a bump in the road with Colt, and instead of handling Colt's troubles on her own, she'd called him crying? Her ex had once told her he hated it when she was needy. Ever since, she'd made a point of trying to be independent and strong. But sometimes that was hard.

"That was some stunt that little rascal pulled at the

bank." Mabel removed the casserole from the oven, then took one of her best Tupperware bowls from the cabinet.

"I hoped you would let me sleep on it before drilling me for details."

"Fat chance." Mabel snorted. "News that your great-grandson is a juvenile bank robber spreads pretty fast. Marsh, thank you for helping Effie get it all sorted out."

"Oh—I didn't do much." He leaned on the door jamb. "Just lent moral support."

I appreciated you being there more than you could ever know.

"Sometimes, that's the best help a body can give." She snapped the lid on the container she'd just filled. "Y'all have salad dressing over at the bachelor pad, or should I send that, too?"

"I'm sure Wallace has a bottle of something stashed in his cabinets."

"Ha!" She shook her head, and took an unopened jar of Thousand Island from her pantry. "Just in case, better take this."

"Thanks." Marsh accepted the gift with a smile. "Effie, what time do you want me here tomorrow to take you to your van?"

"Nine—if that's not too early. I'll send Remington on the bus, but Colt and I have a meeting with the principal at ten, and I don't want to be late. Pretty sure my home-grown Jesse James is expelled."

He winced. "Sounds like a fun morning."

"I know, right?"

Mabel finished assembling the care package and handed the loaded brown paper sack to Marsh. "If he's booted from school, that boy should do hard labor."

"Agreed," Effie said. "I'll fill his days with so many chores that school will seem like a vacation."

"Wallace and I have plenty for him to do at our place, too. We'd be happy to take him off your hands for a day or two."

"Perfect," Mabel said. "I want him transformed into a gentleman by the wedding. I have enough to worry about without wondering if one of my ring bearers is up to no good."

Marsh laughed. "Understood. I'll see what I can do."

With dinner in hand, their guest made his goodbyes, then left.

The moment his truck left the drive, Effie said, "Why did you accept his help with Colt's punishment? He probably already thinks I'm a nutcase for having him come to the station."

"Know what I think?" Mabel had a spark of mischief in her eyes. "That man's as sweet on you as you are on him. In fact, Wallace and I both were just saying—"

"You talked about this imaginary romance you've fabricated between Marsh and me with his grandfather? *Why?*"

Instead of answering, Mabel blew her a kiss. "Why not?"

THE NEXT MORNING, Marsh showed up at Effie's five minutes early. Ominous clouds threatened to dump a gully washer any second, and he'd hoped to get Effie and her precious cargo in the truck before the storm started.

He knocked on Mabel's screen door in time to catch one helluva commotion.

"I don't wanna go! The police are gonna get me!" Colt ran out the door. Too bad for him, Marsh was there to catch him.

"Whoa. What's the hurry?"

"Mr. Marsh, *please* save me! Mom's taking me back to jail!"

"Good morning," Effie said.

"Morning." While Colt hid his face in the crook of Marsh's neck, Marsh tipped his cowboy hat in greeting. "Everything okay?"

Cassidy rode her mama's hip. Her eyes were red and cheeks tearstained.

"No, Mr. Marsh, I'm not okay." Colt clung tighter. "She's crazy if she thinks I'm going back."

Lightning cracked and thunder boomed.

The baby burst into tears, as did Colt.

Damn. Marsh forced a deep breath. "Colt, wanna know a secret?"

The boy nodded.

Marsh whispered in his ear, "I know where your mom's taking you, and it's not to jail."

"How do you know?" he whispered back. "Because she said we're going to school, but I don't believe her."

"Well, you should. You have a meeting with your school principal. She's sad about how you acted at the bank and wants to talk to you."

"What about the scary policeman?"

"He won't be there."

"Promise?" he asked with a sniffle.

Marsh nodded.

"Will you go, too?"

"If your mom says it's all right."

"It's fine," Effie said, "but we need to get going to beat the rain."

She passed off the baby to Mabel, then all three of them dashed to the truck just as the deluge started.

By the time Marsh reached the end of the drive, golfball-size hail had begun to fall. The pounding against the top of his truck made an awful racket.

He pulled to the shoulder and Colt scrambled into the front seat to sit on his mother's lap.

"Think it could break the windshield?" Effie asked, cradling her son.

Marsh shrugged. "Hope not, but anything's possible."

"What if the ice hits our eyeballs?" Colt asked.

Laughing, Marsh said, "I thought Remington was the only one worried about his eyeballs."

"I worry, too," Colt said. "But I'm not a big baby and always telling everybody."

"Oh, okay."

There was a certain intimacy and peace to sitting in silence together while riding out the storm. Maybe if their situations were different, Marsh would have held Effie's hand, stroking his thumb reassuringly over her palm. For now, he took pleasure in passing time with her and her son.

When the hail stopped and only rain fell from the still gloomy sky, Marsh had Colt scramble back to his seat so they could resume their journey.

With Colt making *vroom* noises while driving a Matchbox Corvette across his window, Marsh said to Effie, "You were worried about how Mabel would take all of this. Once I left, how did things go?"

"Perfect. She never said a word. Sometimes I wonder if I'm my own harshest judge. Like because of what happened with my ex, I automatically assume blame when in reality, sometimes stuff just happens."

"I know the feeling. Wonder if there's a support group for that? It's-my-fault-aholics?"

Her laugh filled him with warmth and goodwill and a general feeling of acceptance.

All too soon, the truck devoured the miles to town, and he was back in the school parking lot, pulling alongside Effie's van.

"Ready?" he asked.

"Sort of?" Her short laugh and clasped hands gave away her nerves.

"Come on." He indulged his own nerves by giving her hand a squeeze. "Everything's going to be fine. Colt can start serving his sentence, and then things will get back to normal."

"Mr. Marsh," a small voice said from the backseat. "Can you carry me? My legs don't work."

"That's not good." Marsh opened his door and slid out from behind the wheel. "How about I help you down, then we'll figure out the problem?"

"Okay…"

By the time Marsh walked around the truck, Effie had already opened Colt's door and unbuckled his seat belt.

The storm had passed save for the black clouds off to the east. Filtered sun made grass especially green. Front-range peaks had gotten snow.

"See?" Colt flopped his legs. "They don't work."

Marsh scooped him up and out, planting him firmly on the blacktop.

"It's a miracle," Effie teased before taking his hand. "I'm so relieved."

"You hold my hand, too." Colt thrust out his arm toward Marsh.

"Please," Effie coached.

"Pleeeease," Colt said with a jump.

They walked as a trio to the school's main entrance, but then Effie pulled back before going inside. "Colt, I'm worried you're not taking this seriously. You made a bunch of very bad decisions at the bank, and I'm afraid you think this is all a joke."

"I don't, Mom." Colt shook his head. "I'm gonna be *real* good forever! Mr. Marsh is gonna help, right?"

"Sure," Marsh said. "But listen to your mom."

He and Effie shared a look that made him feel like an integral part of her son's team. When she smiled, pride swelled in his chest.

Effie signed in with the school secretary, then they waited outside the principal's office.

Funny how even though Marsh had done nothing wrong, his clenched stomach told him he was right back in hot water himself. School even smelled the same—like old books and pink erasers and crayons.

"Last time I was in this position," he whispered to Effie, "I'd just pitched about five water balloons on the school bus."

Effie shook her head and held her finger to her lips. "Don't give him any ideas."

Those lips… Little did she know, she was the one giving him seriously bad ideas—like leaning in to steal a kiss.

"Mrs. Washington, Colt—Principal Foley is ready for you."

Introductions were made, with Marsh being labeled as a family friend, then Colt sat between Effie and Marsh. He looked small in the grown-up chair, but held his chin high. Would he learn from this experience or revert to his mischievous ways?

"Colt." The stern-faced woman removed tortoiseshell-rimmed glasses and set them on her desk. "I've been principal of this school for fifteen years. I like to think in that time I've seen everything, but I'm still floored by the chaos you caused."

As if he only understood a fraction of what she'd said, Colt cocked his head.

"This school has had an excellent relationship with First State Bank for many, many years. Now, because of what you did, no students will ever be allowed to tour again. How does that make you feel?"

"Bad." He hung his head.

"How do you think I felt when police questioned me and your teacher, asking us if we'd asked you to take that money? I was mortified. So was Mrs. Logan, and I'm sure your mom. You're old enough to start thinking of others when you make decisions."

"What does that mean?" Colt asked.

"Excellent question." She leaned forward, bracing her forearms on her desk. "Let's say you're in the lunchroom and decide you don't like green beans. You then decide since you don't like the beans, the best place for them to be is on the floor. Sound familiar?"

"I did that…"

"Yes, Colt, you did."

"Why wasn't I told?" Effie asked.

"His teacher sent a note home," the principal said.

All eyes shifted to Colt. He started crying. "I threw the note out the bus window to see if it would fly!" He made a stab at leaping up from his chair, but Marsh's reflexes were quicker, and he held him down.

"Not so fast, buddy. We're not running from problems anymore. We're going to face them head-on—like a man. Okay?"

Colt nodded.

The principal cleared her throat. "When you threw your beans on the floor, you didn't know it, but you started a chain reaction. You might have scooped up those beans with a napkin, but later that night, the janitor had to scrub extra hard on that spot on the floor. What if the nice lady who cooked those beans saw you throw them on the floor? Do you think that would've hurt her feelings? Maybe she felt bad the whole rest of her day. Do you see what I mean? When you behave inappropriately, you're not the only one affected. Just like our country and state and town, our school is a community. We all need to help each other do better—not worse. Do you understand?"

"Kinda," Colt said.

"Thank you for your honesty. If I used big words, maybe later your mom or her friend Marsh might help you understand."

"Of course," Effie said.

"Good. Now, on to your punishment. Since we've never had anything quite like this happen, your teacher and I weren't sure how best to handle it. You've broken a number of school policies, so first, you will not be allowed on any further class field trips for the rest of the year. Second, you will be suspended from class for all of next week. Your teacher will give your assignments to your mother, and you will be expected to do all of your work. Third, with your mother's help, you will write an apology letter and, considering your age, compose an appropriate drawing, explaining how sorry you are to have caused so much trouble. I've had the school secretary draw up a behavior contract for you to sign, and for the rest of your time at our school, I will expect you to follow it." She slid a piece of paper across the table, then read the document that she had him write his name on.

Marsh didn't figure the little guy had a clue what was going on, but he gave the principal props for making it all scary and official.

Once Colt painstakingly wrote his name, the principal asked her secretary to make him a copy, handed it to him and then they were excused.

In the hall, Colt saw his class lined up for a visit to the school library. Marsh stood by, ready to snag him if he started to make a run for his friends, but to his credit, he didn't, and they were soon back at the vehicles without incident.

"Thank you for coming—yesterday and today," Effie said.

"Glad I could help." He wasn't ready to leave them. "Want to grab a late breakfast or early lunch? My treat?"

"Yeah! I'm starving!" Colt jumped in approval.

"I'd love to," Effie said, "but judging by this guy's reaction, I should probably pass and get him straight to work. I don't think he should be rewarded for getting kicked out of school."

"Good point." Even though Marsh knew she was right, that didn't make him any happier about seeing them go.

Chapter Twelve

Saturday morning, Effie took care with her makeup and hair. She told herself the reason she wanted to look extra nice was for her grandmother's benefit. Nobody wanted their maid of honor looking like a hobo while shopping for a wedding dress. But honestly, she couldn't wait to see Marsh again.

He'd been a rock through the entire bank incident, and so far, Colt had done his chores and school lessons without complaint. He was like a new child, and when he'd done an exceptional job of cleaning the chicken coop, then asked her if she thought Marsh would be proud, her heart grew two sizes.

The plan was for everyone to ride into town in her van, then trade it in for the new SUV. She still didn't feel great about having Wallace pay for her new ride, but when winter rolled around, she sure would welcome four-wheel drive.

Marsh and Wallace arrived at Mabel's by nine thirty, and by ten they realized that four adults, two boys and a baby and all of her gear wouldn't be a comfortable fit.

"Marsh," Wallace said, "how about you and Effie take your truck? Now that I got my license back, Mabel and I can handle the kids."

"You're sweet to offer, Wallace," Effie said, "and no

offense, but with your driving track record, I'd feel better if you weren't behind the wheel."

"We'll be fine." Mabel shoved her toward Marsh. "You have my solemn vow that Wallace will drive under the speed limit the whole way."

"That wasn't at all suspicious," Effie said a few minutes later while climbing into his front passenger seat. "My grandmother fancies herself to be quite the matchmaker."

"You're getting that vibe, too? Wallace was all over me for not taking you car shopping earlier—alone."

"Maybe the wedding has our grandparents wanting to spread their love bug?"

"Maybe?" He turned onto the county road that was slightly less bumpy. "Shoot, I can't even remember the last time I was on a date. I wouldn't even know what to do."

"I hear you. Mine would have been with my ex, and the only place he ever took me besides a rodeo was Dairy Queen."

"Big spender, huh?"

Effie laughed. "Oh—he claimed he forgot his wallet, so I ended up having to pay."

"Ouch. Was that when you were in nursing school?"

"Yes." How had he remembered? "Pretty sure my parents are still mad at me for dropping out."

"Do you see much of them?"

"Not as much as I'd like. We talk at least once a week on the phone. I'm excited for you to meet them. They'll be at the wedding."

"Nice. My parents will, too."

"It's crazy to think that once Mabel finds her wedding dress, all the planning will be done." She angled to better face him. "I wanted to throw her a shower, but she said she already has everything she needs."

"What about a bachelorette party with all of her bridesmaids and square dancing friends?"

"That's not a half-bad idea. Although I'm not sure where to find a male stripper in our neck of the woods."

He chuckled. "I'd volunteer my services, but my lack of dance moves would ruin everyone's night."

"Aw, somehow I have a hard time believing that. I've seen your chest, and it's impressive by any woman's standards." Her cheeks blazed. Had she really just admitted to not only admiring his chest, but having sneaked a peek? "Sorry. That came out wrong."

"Sounded good to me." His sideways wink made him all the more attractive, and her all the more embarrassed. "You're not too bad yourself. Maybe we could trade services?"

"Marsh!" She delivered a playful smack to his shoulder. Touching him was a mistake, because the last thing she needed was a tangible reminder of just how solid he was.

"What?" he teased with an adorable lopsided grin. "I think it's a great idea. Swapping would save us both a ton of money. I'm guessing it's not cheap to get a male *or* female stripper out this far."

"True." She returned his smile. No matter what they did together, they somehow managed to have fun. Even during the height of Colt's bank robbery crisis, she'd instinctively known Marsh would make everything better. What did that mean? She'd labeled him a friend, but could there be potential for more? Was that what she wanted? How did she know? Moreover, how did she find the courage for a second chance at romance? "You know, it is kind of nice not having to referee a fight in the backseat or pull over to retrieve a fallen teething ring or rattle."

"I'll bet. Want to try getting really lucky and wrangling a whole dinner to ourselves after buying your car and Mabel's dress? I know a great steak house with T-bones so tender you hardly need teeth."

"Good to know," she said with a smile. "That way, you won't mind if I accidentally leave my dentures in the car?"

"Not a bit."

They both shared another laugh, and as Marsh's truck ate the miles leading to Colorado Springs, it occurred to Effie that he'd in a roundabout way asked her on a date and she'd accepted—of course, whether or not they'd go was contingent upon their grandparents agreeing to watch her crew.

Selfishly, she very much hoped they would.

Nothing sounded better than more time alone with the man who might be her new friend, but whom she felt as if she'd known forever.

Funny how time had a way of either stretching or compacting depending upon the activity.

Effie had been dreading car shopping, but Marsh made it a breeze—of course, Wallace's deep pockets helped, but it was Marsh who helped her understand the benefits of third row seating with an aisle versus bench seats. And it was Marsh who held her hand every time she climbed behind the wheel of one of the monster SUVs. He not only helped her pick between white and midnight blue—blue because it would show less dirt—but he corralled the boys when they'd gotten too rowdy on the dealership's playground. He'd also coaxed a smile out of Cassidy when a sudden wind gust spooked her by blowing off her hat.

Was there anything the man couldn't do?

When it was time for them to temporarily part ways for the ladies to dress shop and the men to visit an indoor go-kart track, she was actually sad to see him go, but beyond happy that Mabel and Wallace agreed to take the kids straight home while she and Marsh stayed in the city awhile longer for dinner.

At the bridal shop, it took Effie a few tries before pulling her new tank between the parking space lines, but once she succeeded, she and Cassidy helped Mabel select five dresses to try.

Tired from the busy morning, Effie was happy to find a sofa for her and Cassidy to relax on while a store clerk helped Mabel with her first selection. The store was straight out of a bridal fantasy with sumptuous white carpet, white upholstery, gauzy white draperies and chandeliers dripping with crystals.

Pink potpourri filled crystal bowls and smelled like a blend of cotton candy and carnations.

Cassidy pointed at the nearest dreamy light fixture and smiled.

"Pretty, huh?" Clearly, her daughter already had great taste.

"I don't know about this…" Mabel left the dressing room wearing a full-length ivory gown with a train long enough to reach Denver. The intricate beading was gorgeous, though. "I feel lost in a sea of satin."

"At least it's a gorgeous sea."

Mabel shook her head, taking one last glance in the three-way mirror before ducking back into the dressing room.

The second dress was stunning. The sweetheart neckline was flattering without being too much, and the skirt was full and floor-length with no train. "Grandma, that's gorgeous. Do you love it?"

Mabel made a face. "The sleeves are a little too short. Shows my chicken-wing arms."

"Stop. You have beautiful arms."

Mabel waved off Effie's compliment to duck back into the dressing room.

The third dress was calf-length ivory satin with a pouf of a skirt lined with layer upon layer of tulle. The top was simple and elegant with a boat neck and three-quarter sleeves. The style looked vintage—like something Jackie O might have worn to a debutante ball.

"Grandma, all I can say is, *wow.* You take my breath away."

"Thank you, hon. If I do say so myself, this one's not half-bad." She actually smiled at herself in the mirror while turning to view the gown from all angles.

"It's perfect. Formal without overwhelming your frame."

"I think so, too. Plus, the clerk told me she has brides-maids' dresses to match. Want to try one on? If you like it, we'll get them for all the girls. We just need to pick a color."

"What about a variation of the burnt orange scheme you've got going? Maybe something like nutmeg?"

"Could be pretty. Let me get changed, and then I'll watch the baby while you find the right size."

"Deal." Effie couldn't remember the last time she'd worn a fancy dress—probably her own meager wedding. Was it wrong if her first thought was what Marsh would think of her in it? She couldn't wait to see him all dolled up in a tux.

Once her grandmother emerged, the clerk measured Effie, then set her on a white velvet dressing room bench to wait for her to bring the less formal version of her grandmother's gown.

"Ta-da." The twenty-something clerk delivered the dress with a flourish. It was pale pink and the sort of thing that was so girlie Effie doubted Marsh would even recognize her. "Ignore the color. We can have them dyed pretty much any shade you can imagine, plus get shoes to match. Oh—and we can also order different necklines and sleeves. Lots of times our maids of honor pick their favorite, and then the other ladies match you or choose their own. It's all about everyone feeling special on the big day, but you'll all have matching skirts. With your facial structure, you'd look hot in an off-the-shoulder number."

"You think so?" Effie eyed herself in the mirror. The square-neck version she currently wore was okay, but she still wasn't sold.

"I'll grab one. Be right back."

"What's going on in there?" her grandmother shouted. "Give us a show."

"Hold your horses. I'm waiting for a different model."

"I'm the bride and didn't take this long," Mabel complained.

"Sorry." The clerk returned, easing sideways into the room. "Someone hung it on the wrong rack."

"No worries." Effie wriggled out of the first dress to shimmy into the second. The moment she saw herself, she knew it was the one.

"Well?" Mabel asked.

"I love it!" Effie emerged all smiles. "What do you think?"

"Perfection." Mabel clapped Cassidy's chubby hands. "Isn't your mama pretty?"

"Arrrgggh!"

"Thank you, sweetie." Effie kissed her daughter's

cheek before turning back to the mirror. Would Marsh love it as much as she did? She hoped so.

"You know," Mabel said, "Wallace and I still wouldn't be opposed to a double wedding. Just say the word and we'll get you your own white gown."

"Grandma, stop. Marsh and I hardly know each other." *Just well enough for hugging, and hand-holding, and wanting to kiss in the worst way...*

"Back in my day, that didn't matter. You grew into a relationship—kinda like breaking in a new pair of leather shoes. Takes years before they're comfy."

Effie shook her head. "You're a pistol. You know good and well what happened my last go-round with a cowboy. Why in the world would I want to put myself through all that again?"

"Because Marsh is better than your no-account ex?"

"True, but that doesn't mean I'm ready to marry him. We haven't even kissed." There went her blazing cheeks. Had she really blurted that out loud?

"Which means you have at least thought about it?" Mabel laughed, then once again clapped Cassidy's hands. "Hear that, baby girl? You might have a new daddy after all!"

Ignoring her buttinski grandmother, Effie removed the dress, handing it to the clerk to finish the custom order.

After an hour of trying on shoes and poring through color swatches, Effie and Mabel decided on a shade called pumpkin chiffon. It was like burned pumpkin, only lightened with plenty of whipped cream—talk of which was making her hungry.

"Excited for your date?" Mabel asked once they'd gotten Cassidy buckled into her safety seat, then themselves settled in the new car.

"It's not a date. Marsh and I are sharing dinner."

"Uh-huh…" Mabel winked. "Bet you at least get that kiss you've been craving."

I hope so…

"Now that we're finally alone," Effie asked Marsh once the steak house's hostess deposited them in an intimate, high-walled booth. "Tell me the truth. How were my boys?"

"Hold up." Marsh grinned. "You get me all excited by telling me you have a question you can only ask when we're alone, then it turns out to be about your kids—not that the twins aren't great, but you know what I mean." He clutched his chest.

"Please accept my most heartfelt apology. I'm deliberately avoiding the serious questions."

"Such as?" He set his leather-bound menu aside to lean in. "Now you've really got me intrigued."

"Before you get too excited, I'm curious if Wallace puts you on the spot the way Mabel does me. She's actually asked if the two of us had considered joining them for a double wedding. Can you imagine?"

They both laughed, but the strange thing was—*yes*, he could all too clearly imagine a wonderful life with Effie. She was the kind of simple, hardworking woman he'd always dreamed of spending his life with. Even better, she already came with a perfect trio of kids. The only drawback? His own shortcomings not just as a man, but as a father. He'd already let down one woman. Who was to say he wouldn't do it again—not by losing another child on his watch, but by somehow disappointing Effie enough for her to pack up her kids and leave him?

Considering that line of thought was a tad heavy for a casual dinner between friends, Marsh kept the banter light for the rest of the meal. He shared stories of how

Remington had beaten them all in go-kart racing, and then how Wallace had run over his best cowboy hat.

Marsh talked about all the things that would steer him from real issues like did Effie ever feel she'd die from being lonely even when she was in a crowded room? Or did she ever wonder if her heart would feel full again? Men weren't supposed to dwell on their feelings, so why couldn't Marsh tamp all of them down enough that he could at least feel normal instead of like a shell of his former self?

They finished eating by seven, so he suggested a walk along the Fountain Creek trail.

The night was perfect. The temperature was just chilly enough to provide relief from the summer's relentless heat, but not yet cold enough for hats and coats.

Marsh knew he shouldn't, but when his every gut instinct screamed for him to take Effie's hand, he did. And suddenly the air smelled sweeter, the river's gurgle sounded like a song and nothing else mattered but absorbing every last shred of peace from the moment—enough to see him through his next dark patch and maybe even beyond.

"I have an odd question for you," Effie said.

"Shoot."

"Well…" She drew him onto a park bench. With both of his hands clasped in hers, she asked, "Is this a date? Or hanging out between friends?"

"Does it matter?" Stupid question. Of course it mattered. But when it came to their individual situations, would a romantic date or friendship change their struggles?

"I suppose not. But I'm just going to come right out and admit that all through dinner, I wanted to kiss you—and that's wrong, right? Because neither one of us has any business getting mixed up in a messy relationship when—"

He tilted closer, framing her face with his big hands. For the longest time, he searched her gaze for confirmation that this was what she wanted. Marsh held his breath, hanging in midair, unsure if it was safe to come in for a landing on her mouth that had taunted and teased for weeks.

She licked her lips, and her pupils widened.

Did he go for it?

What if she'd changed her mind and pushed him away?

Screw it. As a SEAL, he used to be all about calculated risks, and when it came to Effie, he needed to once and for all know if she harbored the same physical curiosities about him as he did her.

He leaned in slow, getting used to the feel of her warm exhalations blending with his own.

A low feminine groan escaped her and he was lost.

He brushed his lips against hers, teasing, taunting, needing this first intimate contact to be a baseline test. He hadn't kissed a woman since his ex, and he was pretty sure Effie was in the same boat.

When he felt the vibration of her breathy mew, he threw caution to the night breeze. He slid his fingers under the fall of her long, lush hair, drawing her closer to increase the pressure of his lips against hers. After a back-and-forth volley of nips and moans and exploration, he parted her lips with his tongue, and she met him for an erotic sweep that made him feel in danger of exploding if he didn't have more.

She crawled onto his lap, onto his raging erection. She slid her hand up his shirt, running her palm along his pecs and surprisingly sensitive nipples.

"What are you doing?" he asked.

"Shh…" He'd started this, but somehow she'd become the aggressor. "Let's find a hotel."

"Eff…" He pushed her back. "Are you sure?"

"Yes. No. Maybe?" She giggled. "All I do know is that my body is craving way more of you than I'm able to get on this bench. I don't want to think about tomorrow, or even later tonight. All I want is to exist in the here and now, for once. If you're on board, let's grab a bottle of wine and a pack of condoms and find a hotel. No strings attached. No implied commitments. Just a night of feeding mutual urges that once they're no longer between us, will make us both more clearheaded and better able to realistically see we're both just a little *pent up*."

"Pent up?" He winked, then shifted to make room for his erection. "I was going to say horny, but for the sake of argument, we'll keep it clean."

She rolled her eyes, grinned, then kissed him again.

They found condoms at a convenience store and made out on the truck seat until the windows fogged. They found wine at a liquor store, made out in a shadowy corner filled with dusty bottles of closeout specials. Then Marsh practically careened the truck beneath a Marriott's portico. "Hang tight. I'll be right back."

"Hurry." She blew him a kiss.

In under ten minutes, he was back to the truck—only Effie and his wheels were gone.

Chapter Thirteen

In regard to the night's wild turn of events, Effie could only plead temporary insanity. If and when she'd even planned on reviving her nonexistent sex life, she sure hadn't imagined it happening in a hotel—even a fairly nice one.

In the shopping center across the street, she spotted a Pier 1, so she slid behind the wheel of Marsh's truck and hijacked it for the brief trip in search of instant ambience.

She found a dozen gorgeous candles and even a fire starter. A few silk throws might be nice to cover lampshades, and spicy potpourri and elaborately beaded and tasseled throw pillows in dusky shades were just the right finishing touches.

The bill totaled more than she spent on a week's groceries, but the more she thought about what she was headed back to the hotel to do, the more nervous she grew—so much so that her hand nearly shook too hard to sign the credit card slip.

Back behind the wheel, she realized she'd left her cell in the truck. Marsh had called thirteen times. Oops. Guess she should have given him a heads-up that she was leaving.

Nerves swirled like a twister through her tummy.

Maybe this wasn't such a good idea?

Her cell rang again, but traffic was heavy and for the remainder of the short trip, she focused on driving. And trying to remember what had possessed her to even be in her current situation.

Marsh's wicked-handsome smile flashed through her mind. More flashes of his ass in Wranglers and the way his biceps bulged when carrying a saddle turned her heartbeat chaotic. There was no denying he was a beautiful man. But she was a single mom with no business getting tangled up in a game of bedroom bingo for a couple of hours when she should be home with her kids!

She pulled the powerful vehicle to the hotel's front entry to find Marsh pacing.

He stormed to the passenger side door and yanked it open. "Where the hell have you been? Why didn't you answer your phone? I was worried sick you got carjacked."

"I'm fine. I needed to pick up a few things, and I guess it took longer than planned."

"That's fine, but..." He pressed his hand over his heart. "Next time you vanish without a trace, would you mind giving me a heads-up?"

"Sure, but then it wouldn't really be vanishing, would it?" She couldn't help but giggle. His intensity was touching—and sexy.

He whipped off his hat and slapped it against the seat. "Hell's bells, Effie, I was scared for you. It's not funny."

"I know. And I'm sorry."

"What did you have to get that was so all-fired important it couldn't have waited till I got the room?"

"Stuff, okay? Climb in, and I'll park."

Though the lot was full, she was lucky enough to grab a prime spot when a couple in a Jeep Wrangler pulled out. She turned off the lights and engine, unfastened her seat belt and then wasn't sure what to do with her suddenly flighty hands.

"Pier 1?" Marsh inspected the bag on the bench seat between them. "I thought you grabbed a toothbrush or something." Upon opening the bag, he made a not-entirely-happy groaning sound. "Candles? You gave me a freaking heart attack for candles? And scarf thingies?" He pulled out the spicy-scented scarves with the beaded trim. "What in the world are these for?"

"To put over the lamps. You know—for mood lighting. I thought it might be nice." A knot loomed at the back of her throat. "It's been a while since I… Candles make everything more special."

"Aw, hell…" He set the bag on the floor, then slid one of his hands behind her back and his other beneath her thighs to ease her in his direction. Once his hands were free, he cupped her face, rendering her incapable of drawing her next breath when he brushed the pads of his thumbs over her quivering lower lip. "Woman, don't you know you're all the special I need?"

He kissed her nice and slow and suddenly everything between them felt fresh and new. Their previous physical explorations had been beyond amazing, but somehow lacked substance. Here, *now*, desire pooled between her legs and she wanted all of him—needed all of him—more than air.

His breath spilled warm and sweet smelling and familiar against her upper lip, and then he was kissing her again and she was falling far deeper than she'd ever planned to go.

Somehow, they made it out of the truck and into their room.

He leaned her against the closed door and kissed her more while unbuttoning her dress and sliding the straps over her shoulders. Though the room was warm and stuffy, the brush of the backs of his fingers against her collarbone caused her to shiver.

"Cold?"

She shook her head before working on removing his shirt.

The room smelled fresh and new and the people next door had their TV turned up too loud. It didn't matter. The event unfolding was primal and a little raw and too far gone to stop. The bag with Effie's candles had long since landed with a crinkle and thud to the floor, along with her dress and Marsh's shirt.

He hefted her into his arms for a quick trip to the bed.

The comforter was downy and white and the parking lot lights spilled through parted drapes, illuminating Marsh as he tossed his hat to the sofa, then braced his arms on either side of her for not just a kiss, but a glorious Technicolor dream.

She fumbled with unlatching his belt buckle and then his fly.

It was no secret he was as turned on as she was, and she gripped him, giving him a squeeze.

"Damn…" He arched his head back and groaned.

She'd meant to giggle, but the sound came out as more a throaty laugh she didn't recognize as her own. In a heartbeat, he'd changed her, rearranged her every goal and priority until all that existed was this moment. The feel of him skimming his rough fingertips over her soft belly and inner thighs.

He helped her out of her embarrassingly utilitarian white bra and panties. Before she had time to worry whether he'd noticed they were shabby from too many washings, he was kneading her aching breasts and placing openmouthed kisses between her thighs.

She shuddered when he moved his kisses higher and hands lower, parting her and stroking her, fueling a fire that had been reduced to coals for far too long. How had she reached a point where she'd forgotten she was even a woman? Now that Marsh had given her this reminder, how did she ever let go?

All too soon, a confusing rush of sensation and emotions flooded her in a rising, building storm. When her arousal reached its peak, in spite of the physical beauty Marsh had shown her, tears fell.

"What's wrong?" he asked. "Are you hurt?"

"No. Yes. I just… This has all happened so fast, and—"

"Then, baby, let's slow it down."

"But I don't want to. Being with you reminded me how deep-down lonely I've been, and I don't ever want to go back to that dark place. But after tonight, we have to, you know?"

"Who says?"

"Common sense," she said through a half smile. "I've got the kids, and you've got the Navy to get back to. Tonight can't be anything more than a temporary respite. But I don't want it to be. And that makes me sad. Why can't I be happy with my lot in life? I've been blessed with three gorgeous children and my grandmother and parents. And you…"

"Come here." He pulled her into a hug. While he stroked her hair, she rested her cheek against his pounding heart. What did it mean that she wasn't alone in her runaway attraction? Was this bond simmering between them purely physical, or could there be something more? Layer upon layer of confusion only crushed her more. She'd already put her children through one marriage falling apart. What if she gave Marsh a chance as at least being a boyfriend, only to once again fail? What kind of example would she be setting for her kids?

"I—I have to go." She bolted upright, giving him a light shove. Even though the room was mostly dark, she covered herself with the throw blanket from the end of the bed. "I'm, sorry. I'll reimburse you for the cost of the room. But I need to get home to my kids."

He covered his face with his hands and sighed. "You're killing me."

"Marsh, *please*."

"Okay…"

She found her panties and bra, then her dress, then locked herself in the bathroom to slide all of it on in the dark, because she couldn't bear to look at herself in the mirror. Finally, sheer logistics forced her to flip on the light, but she didn't recognize the woman staring back at her. Shocker—she looked beautiful. Her cheeks were flushed, eyes bright and hair a tousled mess. She no longer looked like a mom, but like the fulfilled woman Marsh had made her feel she was.

What am I doing?

She sat on the closed toilet seat.

A knock sounded on the door. "Everything okay?"

"Sure." *No!* She was still sexually frustrated and craving more kisses, and after making love, she wanted desperately to fall asleep in Marsh's safe, strong embrace only to wake to find herself still there in the morning sun. But that was just fantasy, and her real life consisted of twin boys and a baby girl who needed her far more than she needed another man who would only inevitably hurt her.

She swiped silent tears.

"I'm dressed. Say the word and we'll go."

He was so kind and respectful. What made her assume that just because Moody had hurt her, Marsh would, too?

"Marsh?"

"Yes?"

"After losing your son, do you ever feel like you're destined to be alone? Like for being stupid enough to make mistakes that solitary confinement is all you deserve? But in my case, that's even worse, because I'm surrounded by little people who need me—are worthy of me—constantly being at my best."

"Come out of there. I want to show you something."

She rose to meet him at the door.

In the room's cramped entry, he took her hand, then led her to a sofa. He turned on a side table lamp before removing three photos from his wallet. He fanned them for her to see.

The first was of an infant, swaddled in blue. "This is Tucker on the day he was born. Leah had a rough delivery and fussed about his head being misshapen, but I thought he was the most spellbinding creature I'd seen in this world. I—" His voice caught, and Effie's heart ached for him. "Before having my son, I don't think I ever really knew what it was like to love. I mean, I loved my wife, but it was different. What I felt for Tucker was all consuming—but in a great way. He made me strive for not just better, but perfection as a husband and father."

The second image was of a towheaded boy blowing out two candles on a chocolate cake that he'd already managed to partially wear on his cheek.

Marsh forced a breath. "By the time Tucker was two, I had this parenting thing down. With the same precision I used for studying military maneuvers, I researched everything from child psychology to the healthiest snacks to toys that were both safe and enriching. When my wife gave him a GI Joe for his second birthday, I snatched it away, biting her head off for giving him a gift that wasn't age appropriate. The look on her face right after I called her out in front of our family and friends wasn't cool. She brushed it off like nothing had happened, but deep down—" he patted his chest "—I knew I could have handled it a dozen more kind ways."

The third image was of a three-year-old running to catch a Frisbee on the beach. His hair had grown longer and darker and his smile reminded Effie of Marsh's. "This photo was taken about thirty minutes before Tucker died. He was playing Frisbee with the older son of one of our friends. The kid overthrew the Frisbee—no big deal, you know?" Silent tears streamed down Marsh's cheeks. Effie yearned to comfort Marsh, but in the same breath suspected this story was something he needed to get out. "It skipped into the water and Tucker chased after it. That particular beach was known for its pristine sand and isolation from the tourists, but it also had nasty riptides, so I'd warned him not to go out past his knees. Even for a little guy, he was a strong swimmer—I made sure of that. After all, he'd grow up to be a SEAL, right? Just like his old man?"

He choked on a teary laugh. "It was near sunset, and the wind was blowing a good fifteen knots. I was having a bitch of a time starting a driftwood fire for hot dogs, and my buddies Rowdy and Grady were razzing me for screwing it up. I was so intent on proving them wrong that I didn't see Tucker run into the water. Leah had been asked to be in her best friend's wedding and was ogling bridal magazines with a few other women. By the time I got the fire started, this kid named Benji wandered over to report that he couldn't find Tucker. I freaked. I ran into the water, but it was already too late. My son floated in the surf like flotsam. I carried him to shore, gave him mouth-to-mouth and CPR. My wife called 911, but he was too far gone for any of that. My most precious possession was already taken. But here's the thing…"

He sniffed, swiping at still-tearing eyes. "Tucker never was a possession, but a precious gift. All along, I didn't get that. I was careless, and those few minutes of neglect cost *everything*."

"Oh, Marsh, no…" Effie drew him to her, and now she was crying while he sobbed against her chest. "Honey, what happened was an accident. A horrible, tragic, unfathomable freak of nature thing that could have happened to anyone."

"But it wasn't just *anyone* who lost their son, Eff. It was me. And now—at least, until tonight, with you—I've felt like an empty shell. No—it was sooner than that. The first time I thought the future might actually be doable was when your Remington was having fits about his eyeball falling out. That cracked me up. I'd forgotten how funny kids can be, and being around your boys and baby Cass feels good. Almost meant to be. Then, there's you. You're comforting and nurturing and all at the same time one hundred percent woman. I can't pinpoint how or when it happened, but Effie, I'm falling for you—all of you—and part of me feels guilty for wanting to once again be happy. For letting my son die, I never deserve to smile again."

"Marsh, no. Tucker wouldn't want you to live your life miserable and alone." But then if that were true, by her own logic, shouldn't the same rationale apply to her own situation? Moody had long since moved on. Why couldn't she?

Why *shouldn't* she?

"We're quite a pair, huh?" He held her as if she were a lifeline, and she held him right back.

"Yeah. So what are we going to do?"

"For now?" He kissed the crown of her head. "I guess get you home. After that, I don't have a clue."

Effie no longer wanted to go home. She wanted to stay.

To climb back into that huge, pillowy bed and cuddle and talk and hold and be held. She wanted to finish what she and Marsh had started. She wanted to feel him—all of him—deep inside her. But what did he want? For even though he'd shared what had to have been some of his darkest secrets, in the grand scheme of things, what did that really mean? It brought them no closer to a resolution on issues she didn't even fully comprehend.

IT WAS A moonless night, and for Marsh, the long drive to Effie's was made all the longer by the concrete silence between them. They hadn't passed a car or house in miles. The isolation was as unsettling as it was complete.

The sensation was akin to a night dive, plunging headfirst into inky unknown, not wanting to go forward but knowing your only other option was to go back, which was really no option at all.

"Are we good?" she asked a few miles from their shared dirt road.

"Sure."

"I don't feel like it." Her voice struck him as sad.

"What do you want me to do?" He didn't mean to sound short, but the night had been rough—physically and emotionally. Why had he shared so much? Why did he now feel naked and raw? As if she could see straight through to his soul?

"Nothing. Sorry I said anything."

In the dash's dim lights, he saw her turn away.

"Aw, Eff…" He turned onto their road but stopped short for an armadillo waddling across the dirt.

They both stared at the tottering critter, then back at each other to laugh.

"I'm sorry," she said.

"No, I'm sorry. I took things too far, too fast, and you weren't ready."

"Oh—but I was ready, but felt guilty about it. Like some harlot who couldn't wait to jump your bones."

"Trust me—" he laughed "—I wanted my tired old bones jumped."

"What are we going to do?"

"For starters, how about we both stop overanalyzing every little thing and just see where our days—or nights—take us?"

"I could do that." She unfastened her seat belt to cozy against him.

He pulled the truck to the deserted road's shoulder and killed the engine in favor of resting his hands on more satisfying curves than the steering wheel.

Kissing her felt so damned good. She mewed against him and damn if they weren't right back where they'd started with him straining his fly and her grinding against him.

He slid his hand up under her thin cotton dress, all too easily finding himself once again fingering the moist haven between her legs. She came just as fast, only this time, when she worked off his belt buckle and then lowered his fly, she whispered in his ear, "Still got those condoms?"

Hell, yeah.

After some fumbling and laughing and sharing the general awkwardness stemming from groping in the front seat of a pickup as opposed to a nice, soft bed, he lifted her on top of him and then slipped into home. Though it had been a while for them both, their bodies moved on pure instinct to the age-old rhythm.

He didn't last long, but then neither did she. When the act was done, she clung to him, and he to her, and with their heavy breathing fogging the windows, for once in a very long time, he felt almost whole.

"What are you doing to me?" Effie rested her forehead against his.

"Likewise. Is this going to be a problem? Because honestly, I'm still craving more."

She giggled. "Me, too. But I have church early in the morning."

"Honey." He kissed her again full on her gorgeous lips. "I don't think this sort of activity would be a welcome topic of conversation in your Bible class."

"Me, neither."

"All right, so for now, let's get you home, then worry about tomorrow when it comes."

"Deal."

Only they ended up using a second condom before he was veering his truck back on the road. Good thing that armadillo was short, or he'd have gotten quite a show.

THE LAST THING Effie expected was for Wallace and Marsh to end up sharing a church pew with her, Mabel, the twins and Cassidy, but now that they were, focusing on the sermon was an impossibility.

The sermon topic was on the importance of truth, which reminded Effie of her white lie that morning when Mabel had asked what kept her and Marsh out so late. A flat tire had sounded better than doing it on the side of the road.

Just driving past the scene of their crimes had reddened her cheeks to the point that her grandmother asked if she was coming down with a cold.

Now, with Cassidy having fallen asleep on Marsh's shoulder and the boys coloring in their Sunday school activity books on either side of him, she figured if the pastor could see inside her guilty heart, he'd have given her a real talking-to. Not only had she lied to Mabel, but to Marsh and most especially to herself.

When she'd told him what happened between them was no big deal, nothing could be further from the truth. Oh, at the time, she'd wanted to believe she could be the sort of woman for whom casual sex was the norm, but here, in the light of day, she realized the gravity of what she and Marsh had done.

All the little things they'd shared had a cumulative effect—from simple walks in the park to working with the boys to that day at the police station when he'd been her rock. Now, when Colt took Marsh's hat from the pew to plant it lopsided on his own head, her heart squeezed in a not entirely unpleasant way. When he caught her staring, he winked and then grinned, and she was lost.

No, they most definitely hadn't just had sex—well, maybe he had—but from her point of view, they'd made love. But she couldn't love him, could she? That sort of thing took time, and she'd known him barely a few weeks.

The sermon thankfully ended, and Marsh hefted sleepy Cassidy onto his shoulders, keeping one hand securely on her while holding Remington's hand. Colt, still wearing Marsh's hat, trailed behind while humming their last hymn.

"You're looking mighty fetching this morning, Miss Mabel." Once they all stood on the small white chapel's lawn, Wallace stole a kiss from his betrothed. The day was sunny and warm with the sky a fathomless blue. It was the kind of perfect day that made a body believe anything possible—especially in the presence of a guy who made her tingle clear from her head to her toes.

"Thank you," Mabel said with a big smile. "You don't look so bad yourself. You could have knocked me over with a feather when you and your strapping grandson showed up. I thought you don't care for preaching?"

"I don't." He kissed her again. "Marsh decided he needed some, but what I really think is that he just wanted an excuse to see your Miss Effie and her brood." He nodded to the small playground where Marsh helped Cassidy into an infant swing while the boys played with their friends on the slide.

"I think you're right," Mabel noted with one of the sly smiles she used when she thought she was smarter than everyone else. She nudged Effie. "While you two were slaving over that flat tire, did you give any thought to that double wedding?"

"*Grandma!*" Effie figured since the church cemetery was close, she might as well keel over from embarrassment. "You know Marsh and I don't think of each other like that." Only, they did—at least, she did. But not anymore, right?

She stole one more glance in Marsh's direction to find him pushing Cassidy, who shrieked with the sort of smile generally reserved for bath time.

Who am I kidding?

She'd fallen for Marsh harder than a chubby kid for cake.

Now, the question was, what did she plan to do about it?

Chapter Fourteen

"Why don't you save us all a lot of grief and marry the girl?"

"What?" Marsh sat behind the wheel of his truck, following Effie in her fancy new SUV out of the church lot.

"Don't think it escaped my attention how you moon over the girl and her babies."

"I don't moon."

"Oh, you moon something fierce. Why else would we now be stuck in churchyard traffic when we could be out on the back porch, sipping Budweisers and watching the horses in the pasture?"

"Whatever." Marsh pretended to focus on the mini traffic jam, but inside, he was a mess. Honestly, he hadn't stepped foot in a church since Tucker's funeral. The only reason he had today was because he had to see Effie again—sooner as opposed to later. He needed reassurance that what they'd shared was real.

"Don't *whatever* me. That girl's a bona fide saint, and if you don't tie her down soon, some other two-bit cowboy with a flashier truck than you will."

"Great." Marsh finally made it to the main road. "So now it's not only me you're putting down, but my truck?"

Wallace held up his hands. "I'm just man enough to say what needs saying—that girl adores you, and so do her kids. Ever since Tucker passed—God bless his precious soul—you've been a shell of the man you used to be. But ever since you woke up in the hospital to find Effie by your side, you've been a changed man. It's like you've found a new reason to live, and I don't mind telling you that if she gets away, you'll have no one but yourself to blame."

"Duly noted." Marsh completed the trip to Mabel's, where they'd be having lunch, and couldn't help but wonder if his crazy old coot of a grandfather might be onto something. But then sanity kicked in. He'd already had a family and lost them. No way was he ready to open himself up to that brand of vulnerability again. He was already in far too deep with Effie. What happened in the truck had been a huge mistake—not because he hadn't wanted to be with her, but because now that he had, he wanted to again.

She was far too good of a woman for him to use for sex—not that he would ever use any woman for purely that purpose—although he'd known plenty of guys who would. To Marsh, sleeping with a woman had always been the natural extension of a commitment. As for the fact that he and Effie had only been on one formal date before hopping into the proverbial sack, what did that mean?

They clearly had the hots for each other, but that didn't make a relationship or any sort of meaningful, lasting bond. If anything, it meant the opposite. But he genuinely did want to be with her, and not just in her bedroom. He found himself thinking about her during all hours of his nights and days. He wondered if Colt and Remington were behaving at school, or if Cassidy had learned any new tricks. She'd be walking soon, which meant Mabel's house would need a whole new level of baby proofing.

After the wedding, he'd offer Effie a hand with making the home extra safe—she needed an air conditioner, too.

"You're awfully quiet," Wallace said once Marsh turned onto their dirt road.

"Yep." Marsh refused to look at the spot where he'd pulled over to have his way with Effie.

"Admit it—you're at least considering my idea, aren't you?"

"No. Of course not. A gal like Effie deserves far better than me."

Wallace snorted. "What's wrong with you? You're an honest, hardworking man—"

"Who let his son die."

"Stop. I never want to hear that kind of crazy talk come out of you again. What happened to Tucker was a horrible, tragic accident. It could have just as easily happened at home with him slipping in the bathtub. If there's one thing I've learned over the years, it's that sometimes bad things happen to good people. Ain't no rhyme or reason to it. Just the way it goes. Think about what it does for a man's character to see how he rises above calamity. That's what makes a man a man."

"Like the way you never came after Grandma?" Marsh stopped the truck in the middle of the desolate road. "Or how you let my mom grow up with only phone calls for a dad?"

Wallace's jaw hardened. "If you weren't my blood, I'd smack you clear to next Sunday. I tried every way under the sun to earn your grandma's trust, but she wasn't having it."

"Every way except for going to her."

"Who said I didn't? I spent months on her uppity Virginia breeding farm, kowtowing to her every whim. After a while, a man gets the hint that he's not wanted, so I packed my bags and came back here, where I pined for her till the day she died. Well, I'm tired of being alone, and since the good Lord has seen fit to still have life in my body, I figure why not spend what time I have left with a woman who actually enjoys my company?"

"Sorry…" Marsh rested his forehead against the wheel.

"You should be, but I'll forgive you on account of the fact that you've been a walking wound ever since losing your son."

"I'm done with this topic." Marsh fisted his hands on his knees.

"Why? Because his memory hurts? Of course it does. But if you'd for one second consider how good it might feel to become a father all over again to Effie's two boys and her baby girl, your life might actually have a happy ending."

"Please, hush." His head hurt so bad there was ringing in his ears. "I know you mean well, but I don't want to hear another thing about me substituting someone else's children for my own."

"But that's the thing—if you and Effie married, her kids would become *yours*. Don't you see? It's the perfect plan."

"Right." All Marsh saw was that his grandfather's grand new romance had messed with his head. "Look, I'm happy for you and Mabel—really, I am. But man to man, back off on your matchmaking routine. I'll be first to admit that Effie's a great gal, but the two of us as a couple just isn't going to happen."

To prove it, Marsh dropped his grandfather at Mabel's front door, then left. He needed time alone—for what, he wasn't sure. All he knew was that talk of marriage made him antsy, and he needed an escape.

"Grandma, stop." Effie slammed the rolling pin she'd been using for biscuit dough on the counter. "For the last time, Marsh and I aren't even a couple, so why in the world do you keep bringing up this ridiculous double wedding idea?"

"Because neither of us is getting any younger, and I don't want you ending up old and alone like me."

"But you're getting married in a few weeks. Your own logic doesn't even make sense."

"There you go again with your sassy mouth." Mabel took milk from the fridge.

Cassidy went wild on her walker, pressing the noisiest buttons as fast as her chubby little hands could move.

Effie sighed.

"Mom!" Remington banged his way through the kitchen's screen door. "Colt found another scorpion and put it in a shoe box!"

Looked as if it was going to be one of those days...

"Where is it?" she asked Colt after a brief march across the yard.

"Snitch!" Colt called to his brother. Thank goodness he at least handed over the box.

Effie cautiously lifted the lid to find one of the biggest scorpions she'd seen in a while. *Ew.* Of course she could dispense of the creature on her own, but how nice would it be if Marsh were around to do it for her?

The thought had been as quick as it was unexpected. Was Mabel's constant needling starting to get in her head?

"Can I at least throw it over the fence?" Colt asked.

"Why didn't you do that in the first place? Why in the world would you want to keep a dangerous animal?"

"I didn't. I just wanted to show Mr. Marsh. Then I was gonna let him go."

"Oh." Effie held her hand over her heart. See? This was precisely the reason why she'd been avoiding forming any real attachment to her handsome neighbor. The last thing she wanted was for her boys or Cassidy to look forward to Marsh being in their lives, only to have him one day vanish like their father. "Well, he'll be here for lunch any minute, so I guess let's put the box on the front porch, and as soon as he gets here, show him the scorpion, then let it go."

"Okay! Thanks, Mom!" Colt raced to the front of the house with his brother hot on his heels.

Effie had just returned to biscuit duty when Marsh's familiar black pickup turned in to the drive. A rowdy bunch of butterflies took flight in her belly. Would she and Marsh manage to grab a few moments alone? If so, would he kiss her? Was it wrong that she hoped he would?

Half groaning, half giggling, she straightened her hair and apron, then dashed to see him. The biscuits could wait. She needed to know if he was as excited to see her as she was to see him.

Effie rounded the corner of the house only to get a bitter reality check. Wallace stood chatting with the boys, but Marsh drove off. *Where's he going?*

Mabel crossed the porch to meet Wallace for a smooch. She held smiley Cassidy in her arms.

Jealousy stabbed every stupid butterfly in Effie's belly. She should have known better than to get her hopes up.

"Where's Marsh going?" Mabel asked.

"He's in a mood."

"I wanted to show him my scorpion." Tears shone in Colt's big brown eyes. "Is he coming back?"

"Don't know, little buddy. But you can sure show me."

"Okay." He didn't look half as excited to show Wallace as he had been to show Marsh.

Effie wasn't sure what to think about this development. Marsh had seemed fine at church. They'd shared smiles, and as usual, he'd been great with the kids. Was he sick? If not, how could his mood have changed on a dime? Was it thoughts of spending the afternoon with her that made him turn his truck around?

That realization made her sick.

"Effie, hon," Mabel said, "why don't you hop in your fancy new car and run after him?"

"No." She'd never been the sort of woman to chase a man, and she sure wouldn't start now. If Marsh didn't want her, so be it. They'd shared one hot night, and apparently he'd found it lacking, or—

Her stomach clenched to hear a revved engine, then she saw him pulling into the drive in a plume of dust.

"Marsh!" Colt ran toward the truck.

Remington followed. "Look what we found!"

"I found him," Colt argued.

Marsh emerged from the truck to greet both boys, then locked stares with her. His intensity stole what precious little remained of her breath.

"Look what's in the box!" Colt said. "I was real sad when I thought you weren't coming, but then you did, so I'm happy!" He dived in for a hug, but in the process dropped the box. The scorpion plopped out at Marsh's boot-covered feet.

"Mr. Marsh, watch out!" Colt cried. "Don't die if he bites you."

"I'll do my best." Marsh wore cowboy boots, as did the boys, so even though the nasty critter looked ready to strike, Marsh could have easily stomped it. Instead, he calmly picked up the box, then scooped the scorpion back in. "There we go. Now, what does your mama want you to do with him?"

"We throw 'em over the back fence," Remington said.

"Sounds good. Let's get it done." He shared another look with Effie before charging off with the laughing boys.

"Looks like somebody missed your mommy enough to turn around." Mabel gave Cassidy a jiggle.

"Grandma, please. Give it a rest." Unsure what to do about her racing heart, Effie took the baby and entered the house. It was far too warm outside—not that it was much better inside. Just one look at Marsh made her feel all hot and sweaty and flushed.

She walked straight her room and turned on the box fan perched in the open window.

Cassidy giggled in the sudden breeze.

"Feels better, doesn't it, sweetie?"

Her daughter cooed.

"I love you. Why does Mr. Marsh make me feel young enough to be your high school sitter instead of your mom?"

"I'd like the answer to that."

She glanced over her shoulder to find Marsh filling the open door. She gulped, holding Cassidy tighter.

"It's hotter than you know what in here." He removed his hat to fan himself. "You ladies mind sharing your breeze?"

"Where were you?" Effie blurted after making room.

He sighed. "Needed time to think."

"'Bout what?" Her heart hammered.

"I think you know." He stepped forward, easing his hand under the fall of her hair. He brushed his thumb over her lower lip, and she closed her eyes, leaning in to his touch, yearning for more, fearing it wouldn't come.

Her breath hitched. "I—I really don't."

"What happened last night—I know we agreed it was

no big deal. Just physical. But for me it was more. And I need to know—"

"It was for me, too." She bridged the gap between them, shifting the baby farther back on her hip to allow space to press her lips to his. "But I'm scared. I'm not ready for anything serious, but part of me feels like we're sort of accidentally already there."

"Ditto." He laughed. "So what are we going to do about it?"

"Who says we have to do anything?" She looked down, then up. "Except maybe share more of these…" Kissing him again felt like the most natural thing in the world, as if there'd never been any man for her other than him. Which was confusing, yet at the same time liberating. She needed a fresh start—she deserved one. How could something that felt so right between her and Marsh be wrong?

"Lord…" Even when they'd paused for air, he still held her. "I never expected this. To feel…"

"I know. Me, too." He looked as perplexed by the emotions swirling between them as she felt. "But that's okay. We have all the time in the world to figure out what we want to do."

"True. But here's the thing. On the way over, Gramps and I got into it. He thinks I should marry you, and I—"

"Oh, no." She stepped back. "Grandma's been giving me the same grief. I'm so sorry."

"What do you have to apologize for? It's not your idea."

"I know, but I'm not some damsel in distress, waiting for a prince to charge in on his white stallion."

"That's a relief." He exhaled, then shot her a sexy grin that flip-flopped her tummy. "All I have is a chestnut and an old black Ford."

"At least it's not a Chevy." She winked.

He rewarded her humor with another kiss. "Here's the thing. As crazy as it sounds, maybe we should make things more official? You and your boys could use a man around the house, and I sure could use a few decent meals."

"What about love?" Her pulse charged off at a gallop. She didn't love him, did she? How could she be sure? She'd loved Moody heart and soul, but look how that turned out. Maybe love was overrated? Old-fashioned? Maybe the excited rush between her legs was more than enough reason to agree to spend the rest of her nights with this man?

He shrugged. "It'll come. Hell, maybe I'm halfway there? All I know is that after church, when I drove away from you instead of toward you, it brought on awful indigestion. Both of our grandparents wasted a lot of time. I don't want to reach their age and wonder what happened to my life. Since the day you saved me from that snakebite, I've seen you as my own personal angel. Nothing would make me happier than for us to move in together, and you be my steady girl."

His steady girl? As in *girlfriend*? Not bride? Effie's heart sank. *Silly rabbit, of course he doesn't want to permanently hitch himself to you.* Moody hadn't. Why would Marsh?

"What's wrong? You look pale. If I'm moving too fast, say the word."

Moving too fast? She was the one who'd assumed he was proposing marriage after having only known her a few weeks. If anything, she was the one moving them along at lightning speed. Considering her misgivings about them sharing anything at all, she should be happy about this turn of events. But the truth of the matter was that she felt as if one of those biscuits she was supposed to have been making had lodged in the back of her throat. She didn't want to be Marsh's girlfriend. She wanted to be his lover and best friend and so much more. But how did she tell him that when even she wasn't sure? And where did her boys and Cassidy fit into this awkward mix? As the mother of three impressionable young children, she wasn't the ideal candidate for *shacking up*.

"I'm sorry. Shit. I misread this whole situation. Forget I said anything."

"Marsh, here's the deal. I obviously like you—a lot. But it's not just my feelings I have to consider. Please don't think I'm pressuring you, but I can't have you moving in here without some sort of permanent commitment. I'd hardly consider myself to be a saint, but…"

"No need to explain. I understand."

Do you? Can you read between the lines to see that in another life, I would give anything in the world to be your girlfriend, but that now, I need and deserve more?

"We should probably get back outside. There's no telling what trouble Colt's got into." He turned to leave the room.

"Aw, Marsh, wait."

"No. I'm good." His backward wave had her worrying her lower lip. At the moment, she was anything but *good*.

"Cass," she whispered to the baby, "what have I done?"

Chapter Fifteen

Marsh worked through the afternoon on autopilot.

He suffered through lunch while sandwiched between the two boys to whom he wanted to be a father. He stood alongside his grandfather, washing dishes while listening to an endless round of upcoming wedding plans. He even changed Cassidy's diaper when Effie's hands were literally tied up with helping her grandmother make rice bag wedding favors.

Initially, his speech to Effie had rocked right along. She'd sure seemed into him when they'd kissed. So what had happened to change her tune?

By "permanent commitment," he assumed she meant no more fooling around before marriage, but he wasn't ready for that huge of a step. He didn't know when he would be—if ever. So where did that leave them?

Marsh had been ready to leave for a good hour, but his grandfather was now engrossed in a Dallas Cowboys game. So here he sat, bouncing Cassidy on his knee while the women played wedding. How different would the day have played out had he done something crazy like asking Effie to marry him? Would he then be looking to this baby girl's future? Knowing he'd be along for the ride?

"Mr. Marsh?" Remington asked.

"That's me."

"Colt wants to know if you want to come ride bikes."

"I would love to," Marsh said, thrilled for the opportunity to escape. "Since your mom's busy, what should I do with your sister?"

"Put her in her walker. She likes it." Remington rolled over the giant toy.

Marsh settled her on the plastic seat, but Cassidy wasn't having it and started to cry. The instant Marsh hefted her back into his arms, save for the tears still shining on her cheeks, her cranky mood was gone.

"Leave her with me," Effie said.

"No way," Mabel said. "I need your young hands for knot tying. Marsh, will you be a dear and keep the baby with you?"

"Yes, ma'am."

"You don't have to," Effie argued.

"What if I want to?" he snapped back.

Wallace whistled. "Would you two knock it off? You just jabbered over my play-by-play."

Marsh ignored the baby's mother and his grandfather to walk out the front door.

"Come on, Mr. Marsh! Cassidy can ride, too!"

"I don't know about that." Marsh winced when he got a face full of afternoon sun. "How about I just watch you and Colt?"

"Okay!" Remington ran toward the barn.

Marsh had just passed his truck when Effie bolted from the house.

"I told you I'd keep the baby." After lunch, she'd changed from her church dress to frayed jean shorts that hugged her derriere a little too well. Her pale blue T-shirt enhanced not only her eyes, but womanly portions of her anatomy that he wouldn't mind revisiting.

He asked, "How long are you going to do this?"

"Do what?" She shielded her eyes from the sun.

"Treat me like a bad guy for asking you to be my steady. I'm sorry, okay? Can we just go back to being friends?"

"No." She reached for the baby, but he wasn't ready to give her up.

"Why not?"

"Because I want more." Hands on her hips, she added, "I'm worth more."

"But by your own admission, not only are you not ready for this elusive *more*, but you might not ever be. Where does that leave me?" The woman's logic made his teeth hurt.

"I—I don't know." Aw, hell. Now, she was crying. "Maybe I do want to be married again one day—just not to an admittedly no-good cowboy like you."

"Exactly." While the boys were still in the barn, he drew Effie around to the side of his truck shielded from the house and barn. Once he had her partially hidden, he nuzzled her neck in the way he knew drove her wild. "Hitching your wagon to mine would be bad."

"Uh-huh…*oh.*" She gasped when he slid his palm under her shirt and up her waist to cop a feel of the assets that had driven him crazy for hours.

Lord, Effie felt good and tasted even better. The lack of blood flow to his brain was making him crazy—or maybe that would be crazier?

Cassidy cooed and kicked against him.

"We shouldn't be doing this in front of the baby." Effie drew back to fuss with her clothes and hair. "Give her to me, and I'll run her inside."

Tired of arguing, he passed Cassidy into Effie's outstretched arms. Even the trade-off caused pressure beneath his fly. This situation was no good. "To clarify—

are you essentially saying you never want to have sex again before marriage?"

She froze. "Did I say that?"

"So basically, I'm good enough to sleep with, you just don't want me around your kids?"

"I didn't say that, either."

"So what did you say?"

"Stop." She pressed her free hand to her forehead. "Your needling is darn near as bad as Mabel's. Bottom line, I guess maybe I am ready to marry you, Marsh Langtree, but all you want is a roll in the hay."

"Point of fact—I'd prefer a roll in your nice, soft bed. But only after I get you an air conditioner."

"You're not getting me anything."

"Actually—" his hands were back on her hips "—I think for once, I'm going to throw caution far into the wind and buy you an air conditioner *and* a pretty ring. Then I'm going to stand you up before God and our grandparents and the rest of our family and friends to make an honest woman out of you. What would you think about that?"

Those eyes of hers that had always reminded him of the deepest part of the Indian Ocean swallowed him whole. As if jumping from a battleship's bow, he plunged headfirst into a terrifying, yet strangely exhilarating new future. Suddenly he couldn't wait to be a husband again. And a father. Every inch of him looked forward to raising Cassidy and her brothers. Was he ready? Hell, no. But was he willing to take his new life day by day to figure it out? Hell, yes.

"You're killing me, Eff. Am I ever getting an answer?"

"All right—yes." Holding Cassidy sideways on her hip, Effie crushed him in a crooked hug, then kissed him. "But don't you dare break my heart—or my kids'."

"Never." He held up his hand. "Scout's honor."

"I'm gonna need better than that." Her stern look pinned him to the side of his truck as if her gaze were a great big tractor.

He kissed her. "As a man, as a SEAL, as a gentleman cowboy, I, Marsh Langtree, promise to never hurt you, Ms. Effie Washington, or your beautiful children."

"I believe you." Her eyes shone, but in a way he hadn't seen before—as if she were projecting happiness from the inside out. This time when they kissed, he detected a subtle change that made all the difference. In an instant, she had officially become his and he was hers, and far from that being scary, it was somehow liberating. "Let's tell the boys."

He took her hand on the brief trip to the barn.

Remington emerged wearing his bike helmet and enough pads to cover damn near every inch of bare skin on his body.

"Look at you," Marsh said. "I'm liking your protection. You look like a knight decked out in armor."

"Thanks!" The kid beamed, then took safety glasses from his cargo shorts pocket. "I got these, too, so my eyeballs don't fall out."

"Perfect."

Colt zoomed out of the barn on his bike. He wore only his T-shirt, shorts, boots and the wind.

"Whoa." Effie grabbed his handlebars. "Where are your helmet, knee and elbow pads?"

"Those are dumb!" He wrestled free and tore off to the end of the driveway.

Remington tentatively followed.

"Colt!" Marsh shouted. "Get back here and do what your mom said."

"Don't have to! You're not my dad!"

"I'm sorry," Effie said. "If you want to back out now, before we make anything official, I'd understand."

"Not a chance." He kissed her sweet lips and Cassidy's rosy cheek before striding down the dirt drive.

"Mr. Marsh!" Remington shouted from the road. "Look at me! No hands!"

"Cool. But take it easy." Even though the twins rode matching dirt bikes well suited for the bumpy road, Marsh didn't feel comfortable about Remington's hot-dogging.

"I'm way better!" Colt zoomed past, holding his hands higher than his brother's.

"Not so fast, buddy." Just past the mailbox, Marsh jogged to catch up with Colt, snagging the bike by the back of the seat. "We need to talk."

"I wanna ride my bike."

"Fair enough, but listen to me first. You just told me I can't tell you what to do, because I'm not your dad. But what if I'm your stepdad?"

Colt's gaze narrowed, and he scrunched his nose. "What's that mean?"

"I'm going to marry your mom, and you, me, Remington and Cassidy are all going to be a family. So how about you ride back to the barn to grab your helmet and pads like your mom asked."

"I don't want to."

"That's not what I said." Starting today, Colt's combative attitude was going to end. Marsh had already made headway, but there was still plenty of room for improvement.

"Are you really gonna be our new dad?" Remington asked. "Like forever? You're not going to leave like our real dad?"

"Nope."

Remington scrambled off his bike to ambush Marsh in a hug. The boy's strength caught him off guard, but not as much as the force of his own emotional walls breaking down. His proposal to Effie might have seemed sudden, but in reality, since the day he'd woken in the hospital surrounded by her and her rowdy crew, his soul must have recognized they were just what he needed to find a new home. Only that home wasn't a place, but family.

His family.

"I don't believe you." Colt climbed off his bike and let it fall to the ground. He crossed his arms. "Just like our dad, you're gonna leave, because you don't love us as much as Mommy does."

"Probably not. *Yet.*" He'd been around Colt enough to know he rarely called Effie Mommy. When he did, Marsh's guess was that he was dealing with more emotions than his little brain could compute. To Marsh's way of thinking, his primary job was to ensure Effie's boys—his boys—never again had to worry about anything other than being kids. "But I figure the more time we spend with each other, the better things will be."

"Maybe." Colt kicked a clod of dirt.

"What do you say? Could you please put on a helmet for your mom? I know you're an awesome bike rider and don't need it, but she worries. You don't want to make her worry, right?"

"I s'pose not."

"Awesome. Thanks." Marsh picked up Colt's bike to wheel it toward the garage.

"Mr. Marsh?"

"Yep…"

"If you marry my mom, does that mean you'll come live with us?"

"Yessir…"

"Can me and Remington's ponies come, too?"

"Absolutely."

"Okay, then. Guess it's all right if you marry my mom."

"Thank you for your permission. It means a lot to me that the man of the house approves—you are the oldest, right?"

Colt nodded, then took off running toward his mom. "Guess what?"

"What?" she asked.

"Mr. Marsh said our ponies get to come live here!"

"That's great, hon. Did he say anything else?" She looked to Marsh. Was she worried about how her boys had taken the wedding news?

"He's gonna marry you and stay forever, but since I'm the man in this house, I gotta put my helmet on so you don't worry."

"Oh…" Struggling not to grin, she nodded. "That makes sense. Thank you. I hate to worry."

"You're welcome."

"Damn." Once both boys were in the barn, Marsh exhaled. "For a second there, I worried Colt might challenge me to a duel, but, knock on wood, I think everything's going to be all right."

"Effie May Washington!" Mabel shouted from the front porch. "What in the world is taking you so long? My wedding's in only two weeks, and we have to get these rice bags done."

"Coming!" Effie shouted back.

"Woman…" Marsh groaned. "Do you know how much I wish I could make that statement true?"

"Get your mind out of the gutter." She might have scolded him, but she couldn't hide her pretty pink flush.

"This all happened pretty fast, but we have a few logistics to go over. First, do you want to join Mabel and Wallace on their big day?"

She shook her head. "Honestly, I'd rather keep it small—maybe just the two of us at the courthouse."

"You wouldn't want to include the boys and Cass?"

"I don't know. I mean, do you think we should? Or is this grown-up business?"

"It's family thing, and honestly, once our moms get wind of our engagement—since they'll both already be here for the wedding—my guess is that they'd both be miffed not to be included."

"I'll bet you're right. But where would I even start? I don't have a dress, and would Grandma's feelings be hurt if I share in her bridal spotlight?"

"Didn't you tell me she'd been harping on you about a double wedding?"

"Well, sure, but…"

"Relax." He drew her and the baby into a hug. "Promise, nothing's going to go wrong." *I hope.* Marsh had made a ton of bold claims in the past hour, but could he back them up? He wanted nothing more than to be the man and father Effie and her kids so badly needed. In the heat of moment, he'd meant everything he'd said— still did. Time would be the ultimate judge on whether this would pan out to be the best or worst decision he'd ever made.

DURING HALFTIME OF Wallace's game, Effie muted the TV.

"Hey, what's the deal?" Wallace complained. "Shakira's about to sing."

Marsh asked, "How do you even know who she is?"

"I might be old, but I'm not dead. She's a looker."

Mabel pitched a rice bag at his head.

"Ouch!" Wallace held out his hands. Warding off a

future attack? "Precious, you know you're the only girl for me."

"I'd better be," Mabel said.

"If you two are done, Effie and I have news." Marsh cleared his throat.

"Yes." Effie put down the scissors she'd been using for the rice bag ribbons. "While the boys are outside and Cass is down for a nap, we thought it would be the perfect time to tell you..." Her mouth suddenly went dry. This was a big deal. She glanced to Marsh for reassurance, but his sexy grin only made her heart pound faster. Would she ever grow accustomed to him being her man? Did she want to? Being awed by him was half the fun of this ride she suddenly found herself on with no seat belt. "Grandma, Wallace..."

Mabel shrieked. "Oh, my stars, you two are getting hitched!"

"I'll be damned." Wallace rose from the recliner he'd bought himself and had delivered to shake his grandson's hand, then hug Effie. "Congratulations, you two. We're going to make this the best damned wedding this state has ever seen."

"You've made me the happiest woman alive." Mabel's hug was even stronger than Wallace's. "I haven't wanted to say anything, but ever since Cassidy was born, hon, you've had a sadness in your eyes that hasn't once lessened until that day Marsh came straight from the hospital to see about his horse."

Effie remembered. But if she were honest, her attraction for Marsh had been piqued while he'd still been in the hospital—when Wallace told her about what happened to Tucker. Her heart had ached for Marsh, yet at the same time she'd longed to help him see there could be a vibrant future worth living on the other side of tragedy. The kind of future that up until now, she wouldn't have believed possible.

"We'll need to find you a dress first thing in the morning," Mabel said. "And Wallace, since Marsh and Effie will want to invite their own friends, do you think we should have more food?"

"That's a darned good idea," Wallace said. "I'll have the caterer make double our original order."

"Slow down," Marsh said. "None of that's necessary. Effie and I will be perfectly happy with a courthouse wedding."

"That's right," Effie said. "We don't want to take anything from your big day—especially with it being only a couple weeks away."

"Hogwash." Wallace waved off her concern. "You two will be married with us, and that's final."

Marsh didn't look so sure. Was he already having doubts?

Effie left her grandmother to take his hand. She gave him a reassuring squeeze. "What do you think?"

"We'll do whatever you want." He said the words, but did he mean them? Or was she once again overanalyzing?

"What she wants—" Mabel slipped her arm around Effie's waist "—is to be part of our fabulous wedding. Right, sweetheart?"

Actually, no. The whole thing sounded overwhelming, but Mabel and Wallace looked so excited by the prospect that Effie didn't have the heart to disappoint them.

"Sweetie?" Mabel gave her a nudge. "You want to be married at the same time as us, right?"

"Sure." Once again, Effie found herself looking to Marsh, only his focus was on the TV, where Shakira shook her assets in a skimpy sequined number. Did he have a straying eye like her ex? Was this marriage doomed before it had even started?

"Marsh?"

"Sorry." He switched focus back to her. "I was just thinking how great you'd look in a shiny getup like that." He pointed at the screen. "When y'all were at the dress store, did you see anything similar? Only with more coverage?" He reddened while pointing to Effie's curves.

"Nope." Effie shook her head. Who knew her groom was a closet fashionista? "But I'll see what I can do."

She'd been silly to worry—about anything. Fate had brought Marsh to her, and no way would it be so cruel as to take him away.

Chapter Sixteen

"Hey, man. Heard through the grapevine you're getting hitched?"

"Rowdy Kingman." Marsh shifted his cell to his other ear. "How the hell did you get that intel?" Marsh and Rowdy had been on years' worth of missions. The guy was one of his closest SEAL friends, but once Tucker died and his marriage ended, Marsh had quit him cold turkey, just like everyone else in his life. He wasn't proud of the fact. That's just the way it went down.

"You should know I have my sources."

"Did my mom call you?" Marsh opened the barn door. It was six o'clock Monday morning, and the boys' ponies needed feeding.

Two weeks had passed, and now the wedding was mere days away.

Rowdy laughed. "That secret didn't last long. Seriously, though, man. Congrats. Me and the boys are happy for you, and we want to come out for the ceremony."

"The hell you do. You and the *boys* want an excuse for a bachelor party."

"You got me. Grady and Jesse aren't too far from you in Oklahoma, and are leaving the kids with Grandma for a long weekend. Cooper and Millie, too—but heads up. He's pissy about you not having called. He didn't even know you were in the state. Wiley and his girl, Macy, even want to come. It's a freak of nature that we can all get away."

"Cool." Marsh inwardly groaned. How had a simple courthouse ceremony blossomed into a circus? If he'd wanted to see his old gang, he would have called them. Rowdy was a good guy—the best. But he had been on the beach the day Tucker died, and Marsh didn't need that kind of reminder showing up on the ranch that had become his safety zone. How did he tell his old friend thanks, but no, thanks? He'd just as soon they all cancel.

"So I'm flying into Colorado Springs Thursday morning. I know that's a long-ass trip for you, so I'll rent a ride. Everyone else is driving."

"Where are you staying? Pretty sure my bride and her grandmother booked the whole town."

"True." Rowdy laughed. "But it's cool. Jesse's folks have an RV the size of Rhode Island. I assume your granddad won't mind if we park at your place?"

"That'll be fine." On the way to the grain bin, Marsh's head pounded. The familiar scents of straw and leather tack and sweet manure that usually comforted him instead brought on a headache. Why hadn't he told his friend no?

Because he was too chickenshit to hurt anyone's feelings.

Kind of the same way he felt about this ceremony. Oh, sure, he wanted to be with Effie and her kids. But he'd never wanted to make a big deal out of their union. He still wasn't entirely sure he was good enough for any of them.

"Awesome. Look," Rowdy said, "the CO's giving me shit, so I've gotta bounce. But I can't wait to catch up. It's been too long."

"Definitely." *But not quite long enough.* Marsh disconnected the call, then pitched his phone at a stack of hay bales he'd been assigned to haul over to the Grange Hall for Effie and her grandmother to partially cover with fabric, then arrange for seating. The task sounded awful enough that he might rather get snake bit again.

He fed the ponies, let them out to pasture with the horses, then mucked their stalls.

The whole while, he couldn't shake the feeling that he needed to talk to Effie about how he was feeling—as though he'd made promises he maybe couldn't keep. He wanted to, but what if he couldn't?

Right now, she'd be busy getting the boys off to school. But later, once they met up to do the hay, he'd talk to her then.

"There you are." Wallace moseyed into the barn. He already held a beer. "Just got off the phone with my betrothed, and we'd like you to plan a surprise for Effie with the twins and their ponies. We think if they rode down the aisle, holding both of our rings, that'd be just too darned cute for words. What do you think? Can you make it happen?"

"Yep." *But don't you think this is a smidge over-the-top? Wouldn't our time be better spent focusing on our vows?* Marsh seriously needed to have that talk with Effie. Wedding hoopla was making him lose sight of his end goal—once again being part of a family.

MARSH'S EYES TOOK longer than he'd have liked to adjust to the Grange Hall's dim lighting, but he eventually found Effie high on a ladder, nailing one end of two orange-and-white streamers to the north wall. Her friend Patricia stood on the floor holding the other end.

Mabel and her crew sat at the back of the vast room,

messing with what he could only guess were part of the table decorations.

Toby Keith crooned about red Solo cups, and the whole place reeked of pumpkin and cinnamon he suspected came from the mounds of potpourri bags resting on a side table.

"There you are," Effie said upon spotting him. "Did you bring the hay?"

"Sure. But how come you're doing all of this so early?"

"With all of Mabel's plans, it'll take a good three days to complete this place and the chapel. Plus, Patricia's been kind enough to throw me a shower Thursday night, and I want time to spend with both of our families when they get to town."

"Right." He scowled. He'd forgotten about his parents being tossed into the mix. "Speaking of which, Mom called my old roomie and told him about the wedding. Hope you don't mind, but him and some other couples we know are coming."

"Why would I mind? That's wonderful." She descended from the ladder far too fast for Marsh's liking. The last thing he needed was for her to get hurt.

Her hug reminded him why he was putting himself through this fiasco—for her. For Cassidy and the twins.

"You do know it's supposed to rain tonight?" he said. "Instead of arranging the bales outside, would you rather I park the trailer under the picnic pavilion so they stay dry?"

"That's a great idea," Patricia said. "If we run short on time, I can always have our yard crew pitch in to help. The PTA moms want to help, too."

"Perfect. Thank you." Now Effie was hugging her friend. She was all teary eyed and gushing and made

Marsh feel like shit for having a lousy attitude toward the event that would forever seal their fates.

He had to talk to her—*now*.

"Babe," he took her hand. "Mind if I steal you for a few minutes?"

"Sure. Patricia, could you please finish? I'll be right back."

"Take as long as you want. I need to check my email."

"Great. Oh—and would you pretty please call Dave at the Pumpkin Shack. He promised to be here two hours ago. Four hundred pumpkins aren't going to unload themselves."

"True..." Patricia nodded. "I'll call now."

"Sorry, where were we?" Effie blasted Marsh with a smile. "You needed to talk?"

"Yeah..." He drew her outside where fall sun had already melted the morning frost. Where did he start? Or did he keep his damn mouth shut and let her enjoy her big day?

Her smile took his breath away. "It's crazy how much has happened in the last twenty-four hours. I feel like this wedding is on steroids. Part of me is screaming, how can I be marrying you when I hardly know you? But then another part of me quietly reminds myself that deep down, I feel like my soul has always known you." She tipped her face up, and he couldn't help but kiss her.

She looked so pretty with her hair in a loose bun. She wore denim overalls that hugged her in all the right places and her red long-johns shirt left little to his imagination. What was wrong with him? Not only was she sweet and smart and funny, but a great mom to her three children. In the short time he'd known her, thoughts of her—of all of the Washington clan—consumed him.

Was this wedding out of hand? Sure.

But would he suffer through?

With her as the prize on the closing end? Absolutely.

"What did you need to talk about?" she asked.

Crap. What did he say? His palms were sweaty.

"Hon?" she asked. "Everything okay?"

"Sure." *Liar.* "I, ah, heard from Wallace that Mabel wants the kids to ride their ponies down the aisle as a ring-bearer stunt. It was supposed to be a surprise, but I'm not sure if either of them is ready to tackle those few stairs at the back of the chapel, so I wanted to run it by you first."

"Oh." She cocked her head while thinking. "I see what you mean. Thanks for the heads-up, but they should be fine. It would be adorable. I mean, who's ever seen anything so cute? I'm sure if you have them practice a few times, they'll be fine. Mabel's got the chapel key. Today's nuts—after this, we're finding my wedding dress. But how about tomorrow you bring the ponies and I'll bring the boys and we'll meet at the chapel? Sound good?"

"Yeah." *No.* But for her, he'd make it work.

Monday afternoon, at the same bridal shop where Mabel had purchased her gown, Effie stood in the dressing room, knowing this dress was the one from the moment she slipped it on. The ivory satin design was simpler than her grandmother's, yet had an old-fashioned glamour she couldn't resist. Strapless, the bodice hugged her in all the right places, making her waist appear smaller. Swirls of beading hopefully gave it the sheen Marsh said he liked.

"As I live and breathe." When Effie left the dressing room to show her grandmother, Mabel instantly teared. "It's perfect. How are you wearing your hair? I think up—and you need pearls. I have just the thing. My mother gave them to me for my first wedding."

Effie wrinkled her nose. "I thought Grandpa was a cattle rustler. And didn't your marriage only last a year?"

"Doesn't matter." She waved off Effie's concern. "The necklace is still gorgeous."

"I'll take your word for it." Laughing, Effie gave her grandmother a hug, glad Wallace had convinced them to leave Cassidy with him and Marsh so that she and Mabel had quality girl time. "Thank you."

"You're welcome."

"I don't mean for just the necklace, but…" Her eyes welled again. "*Everything.* You were right about me marrying Marsh. At first, I wasn't sure. I thought it was too soon. But now I think the timing doesn't matter if it feels right."

"Amen." Mabel's big smile was contagious. "Now, go ahead and change so we can get to the mall. Wallace still hasn't told me where we're going for our honeymoon, but he hinted I should pack a couple bathing suits. First of all, where am I going to find a swimsuit in Colorado in October? And second, who wants to see this old body showing so much skin?"

"Apparently, Wallace." Effie winked.

THE ROCK CHAPEL where Wallace and Mabel would say their vows—him and Effie, too—had been built around the turn of the last century at the end of a box canyon that had been turned into a state park. The chapel's pine floor had to be constructed in two parts to accommodate different levels of its sandstone foundation. Because of that, stone stairs connected the two sections.

Honestly, Marsh didn't figure the chapel's caretaker would go for the whole pony thing, but he and Wallace were old friends, and since Wallace had donated enough money to more than cover the chapel's upkeep for the next twenty years, the man must have turned a blind eye to the unorthodox request.

In the shade of three cottonwoods, he unloaded the ponies from their trailer, then saddled them while waiting for Effie to bring the boys.

The day was warm, and the canyon's sunbaked rocks smelled of piñon and sandy soil.

Even he had to admit Colt and Remington would look darned cute riding down the chapel's center aisle.

His cell rang. He assumed it was Effie, but caller ID showed his mother's image. "Hey, Mom. What's up?"

"Surprise! We're at the ranch, but where are you and your grandfather?"

Marsh explained the pony rehearsal. "Wallace and Mabel are at her place with the baby." He gave them directions.

"Mmm…a baby. Hard to believe you're about to be a dad again with a ready-made family. How does that make you feel?"

"Mostly good."

"Mostly?" She sighed. "That doesn't sound right. Is something going on you didn't tell me about?"

"Not at all. This just all happened fast. My head's swimming—in a good way. Effie and the boys are amazing. I'm just not sure I'm ready."

"You were a wonderful father to Tucker. How could you not be ready?"

"You know what I mean. I should've paid closer attention. I should have—"

"Stop right there. Honey, we've been over this a hundred times. What happened was a fluke. A one-in-a-million freak accident that neither you nor Leah could have avoided. Give yourself permission to be happy. From what Wallace has told me, your Effie is beyond perfection. Your dad and I can't wait to meet her, so let's have dinner tonight."

"Okay, sure. I'll call you as soon as we're finished here."

"Sounds good. Talk to you then."

As soon as Marsh ended the call, Effie's SUV rolled down the blacktop lane. On weekends, the chapel was open for tours, but it was closed during the week, which was good. The last thing Marsh needed while teaching the boys how to ride their ponies up and down stairs was an audience. If he got lucky, the little critters would carry the boys on autopilot through the church, but if one of them turned cranky in front of an audience, all bets were off.

As soon as their mom parked, Colt and Remington hopped from the backseat to run toward him.

Effie followed.

"Mr. Marsh!" Colt made it to him first. His pony didn't like the boy's speed and snorted and bucked in protest.

"Slow down," Marsh said. "How was school?"

"It was okay. I got in trouble for throwing a tater tot at lunch, but then I did real good in art class! Look what I drawed!"

"Drew," Effie said from behind her son.

"That's what I meant." Colt took a folded piece of white construction paper from his back pocket and handed it to Marsh. "Look! It's us!"

Marsh carefully unfolded the paper to find that the boy had drawn him and Effie holding hands. Marsh carried Cassidy on his shoulders and he held Colt's hand while Effie held Remington's—easily discernible by the fact that Remington's eyeballs were on the ground. "What happened to your brother's poor eyes?"

"They got ate by the scorpions! See?" He pointed to

dozens of squiggles on the bottom of the page. Aside from his twin's blindness, the scene was idyllic, with a crude representation of Mabel's house and barn covered by lots of blue sky and a smiling yellow sun.

"This is great, buddy. You did real good."

Tucker used to love to draw. Marsh had a box filled with stick-figure family drawings that he hadn't looked at since after his funeral.

To look would hurt too damned much.

"I drawed, too!" Remington pushed his way into the conversation, brandishing a similar image, only with Colt behind bars. "But my brother's in jail 'cause he's always in trouble. He lost his eyeballs, too, and now you love me most!"

"Aw, I love both of you. Come here." He pulled them into a group hug. Marsh laughed past the knot in his throat. "You two are the best artists I've seen in a long time." *The best since my son died.*

"I'm best!" Colt said.

"No, I am!" Remington argued.

"Both of you are amazing." When the boys started smacking each other, Effie stepped between them. "Except for when you're fighting."

The agitated ponies agreed.

"Knock it off," Marsh said.

The boys stopped.

For a few seconds, pride washed through Marsh. It meant a lot that the boys respected him, but it wasn't cool that they didn't show their mom the same treatment. "Both of you please apologize to your mom for not listening to her."

"Sorry, Mom," Remington said.

"Sorry," Colt said.

"Thank you." Effie hugged them both. "Now, let's

get started so we can get home to your great-grandma. She's got a to-do list taller than both of you combined."

"Whoa!" Colt said. "That's humongous!"

Marsh ruffled his hair, then got both settled into their saddles. Something wasn't right. Then he remembered. "Everybody climb off. I forgot your helmets. And remember our first safety rule?"

"Never ride without a helmet," Remington said.

"They'll be wearing their white cowboy hats for the wedding," Effie said. "Just this once I think they'll be all right."

"Eff…" Marsh crossed his arms. Had she forgotten he'd lost a son to a preventable accident? If Tucker had been wearing a life jacket, he might still be alive.

"I know you're hypersensitive about this issue, but trust me, they'll be fine." She slipped her arm around his waist. "Promise."

Marsh clenched his jaw, mumbling under his breath, "For the record, I don't like it."

"Duly noted. So the sooner we get started, the sooner they'll be safely back in their car seats." She kissed his cheek. "Really, stop glowering. They'll be fine."

He closed his eyes, pinching the bridge of his nose. *Breathe.* She was right. He was overreacting. All he had to do was get through this damned wedding, and then life would be back to his new normal—only better, because he had Effie and the boys and Cassidy to share it.

"Okay, guys," Marsh said, "which one of you wants to go first?"

"Meeeee!" They, of course, both said at once.

"Since Remington didn't throw a tater tot at lunch—" Effie tried her best to look stern, but Marsh wasn't buying it "—he gets to ride first."

"Aw, that's not fair." Colt kicked, which annoyed the

hell out of his pony, who jumped and took off at a gallop. Colt screamed, and Marsh's heart damn near stopped until he got the boy to rein in the stubby-legged creature.

"See?" Marsh said to Effie. "This is why the boys need to always wear their helmets. Especially you, Colt. You've got to watch your temper around this guy." He stroked his mane. "He doesn't like sudden movements or loud noises."

"Okay," Colt said. He leaned low in his saddle to hug the creature. "I'm sorry. I won't do it again."

"Good to know." Pride welled in Marsh's chest. He'd take this as an excellent sign of progress with the boy. "Remington, you ready?"

"I think so? My pony isn't going to do that, is he?"

"Nope. In fact, all you need to do is give him a gentle nudge, just like I showed you, and he'll walk nice and slow right where you want to go."

"Let me unlock the church." Effie ran ahead.

Remington walked his pony to the first set of stairs. "Now what?"

"Show him you want to go forward. He might not like the steps, but just like when we're climbing a rocky trail, he knows what to do."

"I'm scared."

"You can do it," Marsh urged. "I'll be right beside you the whole time."

"Promise?" Remington asked.

"Cross my heart, hope to die, stick a needle in my eye."

The boy flinched. "Don't poke your eyeball! That would hurt!"

"I'm just messing with you." He used to say the silly rhyme with Tucker all the time. It had slipped out as naturally as if he'd once again been talking to his son instead of Effie's. But then what Marsh had to remember was that by this time on Saturday, Remington would officially be his son, too. Every time he got butterflies about the convoluted ceremony and reception, he only needed to remind himself of that fact. One hectic day was well worth a lifetime's happiness. "Let's go."

Remington made it up the three stairs without issue, then ambled inside the chapel's massive door. "Look!" he shouted. "I did it!"

His voice echoed in the towering, stone-walled space, and then all hell broke loose when his pony realized he wasn't outside and had nowhere to run.

He bucked like a pinball machine lever and took Remington along for the ride—at least until the boy couldn't hold on any longer.

"Mommy!" he cried, before hitting the wood floor.

Crack. There was the sound of bone snapping.

Blood gushed in an unholy mess.

A bump was already rising on his forehead, and he was quiet, so quiet. Had he fainted from the pain? Or was he already gone?

Marsh froze while the ringing in his head screamed, *Not again. No, no, no—please God, don't let me lose another child.*

Chapter Seventeen

"Colt!" Effie shouted. "Go get my phone out of the car and call 911."

"Yes, ma'am!" He took off.

"Remington, sweetie." Effie knelt beside her son. "Pumpkin, can you hear me?"

The boy groaned. "Mommy, I hurt. Everything hurts."

"I know, sweetie. Help is coming real soon. Stay with me. You probably have a concussion, so stay super still, okay?"

"Okay, Mommy. Are my eyeballs in my head?"

"They sure are, silly." She sniffed through silent tears. Marsh noted worry in her expression, but her voice was calm and soothing—exactly how it should be given the situation.

Meanwhile, he was a wreck. His pulse raced ninety to nothing and he couldn't seem to hear beyond the constant ringing in his ears.

"Marsh," she said, "could you please get the pony? He looks trapped at the front of the chapel and is probably scared."

"Sure." How could she be so calm? Wasn't she mad or scared or freaked out? He couldn't move. Why wouldn't his legs work? What the hell was wrong with him? All he could do was stare at all that blood...

"Give me your shirt," Effie said. "Who knows how long it will take the ambulance, and we need to get that bleeding under control."

"Sure. Right." Marsh abandoned the pony, which seemed calm enough at the moment, and followed Effie's command. Her voice became his lighthouse. His salvation. Remington wasn't dead. He was very much alive and needing help.

"I don't want to move him, so let's make a tourniquet." Marsh handed her his shirt.

She gingerly slipped the shirt beneath her son's thigh, then wrapped the sleeves around a slim hymnal she'd found in the back of a pew, twisting the fabric around it to use for torque. It was a brilliant field move—one Marsh should have thought of first, but his mind was gone.

"I called the number, Mommy!" Colt returned to kneel at his brother's side. "Love you, Rem. I was teasing about scorpions eating your eyeballs. Please be all right." He fit his hand against his brother's, lying down next to him while being careful not to bump against him. "You can go first at the wedding."

"Love you, Colt." Remington's complexion had turned ashen.

Marsh wrangled the pony outside, then took off his saddle and brushed him before guiding him into the trailer. While periodically checking on Effie's youngest son, he did the same for Colt's pony.

By the time the ambulance came, he watched from the sidelines while Effie explained what happened to the paramedics like a pro. Her nursing education shone through. Seemed a shame that she wasn't sharing that knowledge with the world. He was in awe of her calm. Meanwhile, as he watched her climb into the back of the ambulance with Colt, his insides were shredded.

As if he were talking through water, he heard himself tell her and the two boys that he'd meet them at the ER as soon as he dropped the ponies back at the ranch, but the words didn't make sense. He and Wallace could return for her car later. All that mattered now was making sure Remington would be okay.

EFFIE WOKE FROM a catnap.

It was ten o'clock, and darkness had long since fallen.

Remington had been in surgery for two hours.

The surgical waiting room of Arkansas Valley Regional in La Junta was packed with loved ones and friends. Colt had fallen asleep on Marsh's lap and rested his head on his shoulder. Patricia had taken Cassidy to her house for the night, and Marsh's parents chatted softly with Mabel and Wallace. Remington's teacher had heard about his accident and was with her husband, talking to a PTA mom. Effie's parents were in transit from their Oklahoma home.

The outpouring of affection for her son touched Effie deeply. For ages, she'd felt alone without Moody. Yet all along, she'd walked with friends.

As for whether she and Marsh would still be married on Saturday, she'd let Remington's health dictate that call. His doctor said the break was clean, but it had needed to be set, and since the bone had broken through skin, he'd lost a lot of blood and needed extensive stitching along with an open reduction and internal fixation procedure to pin his bone. Nerve damage looked minimal. He had a concussion, and had already been scanned for internal bleeding in his head. Thankfully, that test had come back clean. Marsh had been right. Both boys should have worn helmets when riding. She'd insist upon it in the future—assuming she was able to get Remington back on his pony.

The Wizard of Oz played on TV, and a toddler boy who belonged with another family danced and hummed along.

She glanced at Marsh and found him staring at the boy. What was her fiancé thinking? Since the accident, they'd hardly spoken. Suspecting he'd feel guilty, she'd told him before leaving in the ambulance that the event hadn't been his fault, but had he believed her?

He smoothed Colt's hair.

His love for her son was plain to see, but what did he feel for her? Would he want to put off their marriage until Remington fully recovered? If so, what would that mean for their future? She was too exhausted to think further than her son having a successful surgery.

"Mind company?" Marsh's mother, Jacinda, took the empty seat next to Effie. From their initial meeting shortly before Remington had been whisked off, she'd struck Effie as a lovely woman—inside and out. Her hug had been long and genuine. She was tall with long dark hair she'd styled in a neat ponytail. She wore jeans with a forest green sweater set and a chunky wood necklace. Her dark eyes matched her son's and had plenty of laugh lines at the corners. "I hate that we couldn't have met under happier circumstances."

"Oh—I am happy," Effie said. "This could have much worse. Rem will heal and soon be back to normal. This is only a bump in the road compared to what your family went through."

"You mean with Tucker?" She raised her eyebrows. Was she surprised Marsh had told her about his son? Why wouldn't he? As man and wife, Effie didn't think any topic was off-limits. "Yes. Losing him was one of the toughest things we've faced. I lost my mom not too long ago, and that was hard, but more along the natural order of things. By my age, I'd mentally prepared myself, you know? But with my grandson…" She shook her head. "How can anyone ever prepare for such a tragedy?"

Effie nodded.

"I can't tell you how excited I've been to meet you. Marsh and I chat—probably more than he'd like." She cracked a smile. "The difference you've made in his life is remarkable. Before you—forgive me if I sound melodramatic—I sometimes felt as if he spent his days marking time, waiting for his own death so he could be with his son. But then he'd mention a funny thing one of your sons had done, or how he got to hold your baby girl, and gradually, layer by layer, it was as if your light scrubbed the grief from his soul. Thank you."

Tears stung Effie's eyes.

"That's funny," Effie said without smiling, "because I feel the same about him. When my marriage fell apart, I ended up hiding at my grandmother's. She'd always been my rock in times of trouble, and this time around was no different. Marsh is the only other person who's made me feel as safe as she does."

She beamed. "Then you love him?"

For Jacinda's sake, because she seemed to need that confirmation, Effie nodded. But did she love Marsh? Marriage was one thing, but love somehow seemed more intimate—the final plunge that signified she'd well and truly left her past in the past and was wholeheartedly ready to move forward.

"Ms. Washington?" Still wearing scrubs, Remington's doctor stood before them.

"Yes." Effie asked, "How is my son?"

"Fantastic. He lost a lot of blood, but we gave him a couple units and he responded like a champ. His leg is set and in a cast—we left a window for wound care. I have a son about his age and took a chance on picking a color for him—red. Do you think that's okay?"

Effie laughed, beyond relieved that the most serious item they had to discuss was her son's cast color. She was beyond thankful that so little else had been wrong. After thanking the doctor, he told her that Remington would need to stay the night for observation, and an orderly would come for her once he'd been taken to his room.

"I'm happy for you," Jacinda said with tears in her eyes. Had the accident taken her back to that dark day when she'd received the ultimate bad news about her grandson? Was Marsh feeling the same? Trapped in a bleak past that refused to free him? "If your boy feels up to it, maybe you can still have your wedding as planned."

"Hope so," Effie said. She needed to talk to Marsh. To make sure his head was in an all right place. Those initial moments after the accident had been brutal. She'd relied on her training to get her through. But what served as Marsh's anchor? Initially, his coloring had been as off as Remington's. In those hectic seconds, had he suffered through losing Tucker all over again?

She looked in his direction, but Colt was still sleeping on him. Marsh rested his chin atop Colt's head while staring into space.

"Now that the crisis has passed," Jacinda said, "I'll have Clive take me to our B and B."

Effie nodded, but inside she couldn't help but wonder if the crisis had truly passed in regard to her fiancé. Or if it had just begun.

"DADDY, LOOK!" TUCKER COULD hardly hold the catfish he'd reeled in with his Snoopy fishing pole.

"Jeez, buddy, he's huge! Great job!" He tried high-

fiving his little guy, but with the five-pound fish squirming, giggling Tucker struggled to stay on his feet. "Do we want to eat him for dinner or set him free?"

"Set him free!" Had there ever been a question? His softhearted guy loved animals and always had the same answer. Soon enough, he'd learn some of the food he ate came from the creatures he adored, but until then, Marsh preferred to keep his innocence as long as possible.

"Mommy, look!" Tucker showed off his catch to Leah, who had wandered to the lake from their campsite. It was a stunning day—temps in the low seventies with the sweet scent of their morning campfire and coffee lingering.

"Sweetie, he's gorgeous. Is Daddy helping you let him go?"

"Uh-huh." Tucker's grin lit his entire face.

Marsh's heart damn near burst from happiness.

This was what life was about—sharing the simple things with folks you love. He and Leah talked about her having another baby—this go-round, crossing their fingers for a girl. Time would tell. Luckily, they had all the time in the world.

"Daddy, help!"

In slow motion, Marsh turned his gaze to his son. The fish was no longer bucking to return to the water, but it had died, and there was blood—so much blood. Crimson covered Tucker—his forearms and cheeks and hair. It was everywhere.

Leah screamed for Marsh to save their son, but suddenly Tucker stood mired in inky water with a tar-like consistency that Marsh couldn't swim through. He tried and tried, but failed. And then it was too late, and his pride and joy, his everything, his son, floated dead with the fish.

"Noooooo!" Marsh cried, but the sound wouldn't es-

cape his lips. The more he tried, the more his throat closed until he clawed at himself for air.

"Sir? Wake up." A nurse shook Marsh to consciousness from the nightmare. "Everything's okay."

Marsh bolted upright. His heart pounded as if he'd completed a marathon.

He glanced from the nurse to the sterile hospital room to the very much alive boy asleep in the bed. By the grace of God, Remington looked normal, save for the huge red cast on his right leg.

"You all right?" the nurse asked. "That must have been quite a dream."

"Yeah. I'm good. Thanks." But he wasn't—at all. And with the wedding only days away, that scared him. Effie and her kids deserved all of him, and clearly, a huge chunk of his soul was still back in Virginia with his son.

"I'll be back." The nurse wagged Remington's call box. "Press the button if either of you need anything."

"Will do. Thanks."

Around midnight, Marsh had driven Effie and Colt home. Remington had breezed through surgery and rested comfortably enough for her to at least get herself and Colt a few hours' rest before he was due on the school bus and she picked up Cassidy from Patricia's.

Patricia's husband and one of his friends had already moved her SUV from the chapel to Mabel's.

It was now 3:00 a.m.

Marsh had told Effie he'd spend the night at Wallace's, then they'd ride over in the morning to spend the day with Remington, but he'd been so consumed with dark thoughts of what could happen to the boy if he wasn't there, personally watching over Remington's recovery, that he'd doubled back.

"Mommy?" The weak voice jolted Marsh to full operating capacity. In a flash, he was on his feet and at Remington's bedside.

"She's not here, bud. But I am. How are you doing?"

"Hi, Mr. Marsh... I'm good... Look at my red leg." He was drowsy from meds, and judging by his loopy smile, was thankfully not feeling any pain.

"I see. Pretty impressive." Marsh struggled to speak past the wall of emotion blocking his throat.

The boy's eyes were already drifting closed.

"That's right, get some rest. You'll have plenty of time to talk in the morning."

Marsh returned to the padded bench seat that ran the length of the window. He needed to sleep himself. Judging by Marsh's nightmare, Remington wasn't the only one needing time to heal.

"BUT WHY DOES Remington get to play Xbox in bed and I have to go to school?" Colt stomped his foot.

"Sweetie..." Effie pressed her fingertips to her temples and rubbed. *I love my child, I love my child.* It was Thursday morning. Remington had been released from the hospital Wednesday night and had slept a lot since, but he was generally in high spirits. Effie had asked if he wanted them to postpone the weddings, but he'd then cried about wanting Mr. Marsh to hurry up and be his real dad. Effie hadn't had the heart to launch the discussion about Moody always being his *real* father. "We've been over this. Until his leg is better, your brother's going to do his schoolwork at home. Since he'll be in bed a lot, if he wants to play his games once in a while between his assignments, that's fine. You, on the other hand, have two perfect legs and need to get on the bus."

"That's not fair!" He crossed his arms and pouted.

"Welcome to my world," she teased, steering him by his shoulders to the kitchen.

Cassidy tore around the kitchen in her walker, beeping the horn far more than Effie's head would like.

Mabel sat at the table, poring over her to-do list. "Seems to me we've about got everything covered. With Marsh's parents and your folks pitching in, we'll be all set for our big day."

"I'm having second thoughts. What if Remington's not ready?"

"Is it him you're worried about or you?"

"Both?" Effie poured Colt's Lucky Charms and added milk and a spoon before handing the bowl to him where he sat next to his great-grandmother. "This thing with Rem has been a mess. We're so lucky he wasn't hurt worse, but the logistics of getting him set up at home hasn't been easy. Toss a wedding on top of that and my brain is fried."

"You're young," Mabel said. "By Saturday, you'll be fine."

Hope so.

"Doesn't Marsh have his bachelor party tonight?"

Effie nodded while fixing herself a bowl of Cheerios. "I think it's been scaled down, though. I was supposed to have my shower tonight, but Patricia offered to move it to a couple weeks after the wedding. That way, we'll have something to look forward to instead of feeling rushed."

"Sounds reasonable. Are you going with Marsh to-night?"

"I'd like to." She sat next to Colt, then used a napkin to wipe milk from his chin. "But he didn't ask me. A bunch of his old SEAL friends and their wives are in town. They have catching up to do. He probably doesn't even want me around. Besides, I should stay here with our patient."

"Don't be silly. Of course Marsh wants you with him. Come Saturday, his friends will officially be yours, too."

"Ever since the accident, he's seemed distant." She swirled her cereal in the bowl. "We've talked, but in passing. It's weird."

"Mom?" Colt squirmed to face her. "Are all aliens green?"

"What?" She couldn't help but laugh. "Where do you come up with this stuff?"

He pointed at his cereal box, where a cute green alien danced with a leprechaun.

"Oh—well, I'd say yes. Definitely."

"Grandma Mabel, do you think so, too?"

"Hmm…" She tapped her pen against her paper pad. "I was out in the barn a few years back and saw a purple one, so I would have to say no. Aliens are not just green, but purple, too."

"Really?" His eyes widened.

Effie laughed. "Put your bowl in the sink and brush your teeth. I've got enough to do around here without you missing the bus."

"Okay." He pouted his way to the sink and then out of the room.

"Relax," Mabel said when Effie couldn't stop jiggling her cereal spoon. "Everything's going to work out fine."

Lips pressed tight, Effie nodded. *From your lips to God's ears.*

"WHERE'S YOUR BRIDE?" Rowdy asked while Marsh fished a second Coors from the cooler. The bachelor party had been set up beneath the pull-out canopy of the RV the old gang was staying in. Grady had parked it alongside Wallace's house and the women had set out tiki torches and made a Tex-Mex feast to match the country music.

Wallace was in his element, flirting with the ladies with Rocket the cat on his lap. "We were all looking forward to meeting her."

"I thought she had her bachelorette party tonight, but turns out she's staying home with her boy."

"Man, that had to be tough. Poor little dude. He's doing all right?" Rowdy finished his beer and reached for another.

"Oh, sure. He's great. You know kids. They bounce right back." *Unless they die.* The morose thought hit from left field and damn near dropped Marsh to his knees. He missed Effie. He needed her but couldn't figure out what to say. How did he apologize for falling apart on her when she'd needed him most? He'd been a wreck after Remington's fall. Marsh was ashamed of the way he'd frozen. She deserved a man who was strong 24/7—so did her kids.

"I'm beginning to think this woman of yours is imaginary," Cooper teased.

"Ha-ha." Marsh wanted nothing more than to down a few more beers, then fall asleep and wake to once again feel normal. But hell, did he even remember what *normal* was?

Chapter Eighteen

Marsh? When a car crunched onto the dirt drive at seven that night, Effie hoped it was her man. The longer they went without talking, the more her stomach churned.

"Who could that be?" Mabel put down her knitting to go to the door. "I don't recognize the car."

Effie finished folding a pair of shorts and joined Mabel. Cassidy had thankfully gone to bed early and Colt and Remington played Xbox in their room.

"It's Patricia." Effie opened the door to be ambushed by three of her PTA friends—and her mom—spilling from the supersized SUV with presents and balloons and a cake.

"Surprise!" they all hollered.

"What in the world?" Effie dashed across the porch to greet all of them. She wore yoga pants and a T-shirt. Her hair was up in a lopsided bun. "I thought we were postponing the shower?"

"We are, but we had to do something to celebrate. Since you two brides will be busy with the rehearsal dinner tomorrow, we figured this was the perfect time to check in on you and make sure you're all squared away for your big day."

"How are you, sugar?" Effie's mom, Melissa, wrapped

her in a much-needed hug. "Holding up okay? You've got an awfully full plate."

"Tell me about it." She hadn't realized how much she'd missed her parents until having them both here. They'd been a godsend in helping Remington get settled when he came home from the hospital.

Once all of the women squeezed into the tiny house, someone turned on a boom box with '90s rock and Colt wandered out of his room to check on the commotion.

Melissa cut pieces of cake for him and his brother, then sent him back to his room.

After champagne and laughing over naughty gag gifts and too many servings of cake, Effie felt a thousand percent better.

"There's your smile." Melissa slipped her arm around Effie's shoulders for a squeeze. "When your dad and I met Marsh this afternoon at the Grange Hall, we couldn't have been more impressed. We think he'll make a fine dad for Cass and your boys, and an even better husband for you."

"I think so, too." Effie beamed. Maybe it was the champagne or a sugar high or the simple joy of being surrounded by family and friends—regardless, she suddenly couldn't wait to meet Marsh at the end of the Rock Chapel's aisle.

But before that, they'd at least have Friday night's rehearsal dinner, where they'd have plenty of time to talk.

I hope.

EFFIE SAT ALONGSIDE Marsh at an endless table in B & B BBQ's private dining room, yet they'd hardly spoken two words. The country music was too loud, and the hard surfaces made conversation with anyone not seated in close proximity nearly impossible. Beneath the table, he'd cupped his hand to her thigh, which was nice, and made her look forward to their mini honeymoon to Aspen—courtesy of her parents, who would stay behind at Mabel's to watch the kids—but Effie wanted more.

Two seats down, Melissa currently had hold of Cassidy and showed no sign of letting go.

"Not hungry?" Marsh asked, eyeing her still-full plate of smoked brisket, beans and slaw.

She shook her head.

"Mind if I have your meat?"

"Go for it."

He picked up her plate to slide the beef onto his. "I'd forgotten how good this place is." He ate a few more forkfuls. "Remington's looking good. His color's back."

"I noticed. If he wasn't getting around so much better, we probably should have postponed the wedding—at least our portion." She glanced to the table's end, where the twins sat with Scotty and a few of their other friends who'd tagged along with their parents. Marsh had rented Remington a wheelchair, which made it easier to transport him wherever he needed to go.

"We still can if you want." He drowned his meat in spicy sauce.

"Is that what you want?" Her appetite was long gone.

"No. I'm just saying…" He ate faster than ever.

"Marsh, if you're not feeling this marriage, you'd tell me, right? You wouldn't go through with it just out of a sense of obligation or because you promised the boys you wouldn't leave?"

"Drop it, okay? I'm good. Want your slaw?" He nodded to her plate.

She shoved it in his direction. "Eat it all."

"Thanks."

What happened to the romantic spark that had practically crackled between them the day he'd proposed? They'd made out behind his truck in her grandmother's driveway. Effie could have kissed him forever. Now, she'd just as soon land a swift kick to his derriere. Why wouldn't he open up to her? Clearly, something was bothering him. Or was she back to overanalyzing, and he was just really hungry?

"Marsh?"

"Hmm?" he asked around his latest bite.

"Do you love me?" *For that matter, do I love you?* In a roundabout way, she'd inferred to his mother she did, but deep down, Effie wasn't sure how she really felt—especially with him now being so cold.

He swallowed wrong, coughed, then reached for his beer. "Hate when that happens."

She was on the verge of asking him again when Wallace stood, then clinked his steak knife against his beer mug.

"Pardon the interruption, folks, but I'd like to make a toast."

Conversations quieted and a waitress killed the music. The sudden silence was a treat.

"Some of you I've only recently had the pleasure of meeting, while others—" he smiled at his daughter "—I've known literally since the day you were born. All of you might think it's silly for an old-as-dirt guy like me to be hosting a great big wedding, but to my defense, I love my Mabel with all my heart and figure what better way to shout that news to the world—or, at least our corner of it—than by hosting a party the folks around here will never forget. Now, just when I thought my heart couldn't feel more full, my grandson and Mabel's granddaughter finally realized what my fiancée and I have known from the start—those two kids are crazy about each other, so we figured why not kill two birds with one big old stone by getting them hitched, too."

The crowd erupted with applause and some awws.

"Guess what I'm trying to say in a roundabout way is that I love you, Mabel. I love you, Marsh. And sweet Effie, I've come to love you and your boys and precious daughter just as much as if you were my own. If the good Lord sees fit, I'll have plenty of time left with all of you. If not, I don't want a single solitary one of you having any doubts as to how much I care..." He teared up.

"I love you, too." Mabel rose to give him a hug and her monogrammed hankie.

Not for the first time, Effie envied the easy romance Wallace and Mabel shared. She and Marsh felt complicated. As if he still had many layers for her to peel back before fully meeting the man in his entirety.

"Kiss, kiss!" the crowd chanted.

Of course Wallace and Mabel were quick to oblige.

Marsh put down his fork and eyed her for an awkward few heartbeats longer than she'd have liked. Anticipation bubbled in her chest until she feared she might pop.

When he finally leaned in to kiss her, he tasted of BBQ sauce and that special something she'd learned to recognize as him. Her body craved him, yearned for him, and despite their audience, she wouldn't have been opposed to taking the chaste kiss deeper. But all too soon, Marsh's focus returned to finishing off her plate.

The only thing she could swallow were tears.

What was she getting herself into? Was it prewedding jitters that had Marsh so on edge? After the ceremony, would their easy friendship return? What if it didn't? How would she survive not only the shame, but the heartache of another divorce?

"Hey..." She looked up from wringing her white cloth

napkin to find him brushing silent tears from her cheeks with the pads of his thumbs. "Stop that. You look too pretty for tears." He kissed her again. This time, with enough pressure to let her know he cared.

A silent, relieved shudder rippled through her. Finally, she could relax. He might not know how to say it, but he'd just showed her what her body had been waiting all week to hear—he did care for her every bit as much as she cared for him. For now, that was all she needed to know.

"YOU TWO LOOK BEAUTIFUL." In the chapel's minuscule bridal suite, twenty minutes before the six o'clock double wedding was scheduled to begin, Melissa held Cassidy on her hip and a fresh tissue in her hand to dab her eyes in the event of a tear emergency.

"Thank you, Mom." Effie had expected to be a bundle of nerves, but she actually felt a wondrous, all-consuming calm. Today was her wedding day, and she refused to let anything bring her down. Her dress fit to perfection and the hairdresser had looped and swirled her hair into a romantic crown of curls. Effie had never felt more beautiful and couldn't wait for Marsh to see her. "I love you."

"Love you, too, sweetheart. I'm so relieved Remington felt up to coming. Looks like your ceremonies will go off without a hitch."

"Not if I can't get this last button done," Mabel said.

"That's why I'm here." Melissa tackled the job. "To help."

"Where are my bridesmaids?" Mabel asked.

"Your wedding planner didn't want you and Effie feeling crushed, so she corralled them into a tent on the side of the building to distribute the flowers and do last-minute hair and makeup touches."

Mabel sighed. "What am I forgetting?"

"Do you have your something blue?" Melissa asked.

"My garter."

"New?" Effie asked.

"Racy underwear." Mabel winked.

"Borrowed?" Melissa asked.

"That's it. I plumb forgot."

"Take this." Melissa tugged a crystal pin from her hair, slipping it into her mother's sassy style. "But I do want it back."

"Yes, ma'am." Mabel winked, then deeply inhaled. "Ladies, are we ready?"

They stood in a circle, holding hands. Four generations of strong women. Effie couldn't help but think forward with a pang to Cassidy's future wedding day. She prayed Mabel would still be with them.

Effie nodded. "I'm ready if you are."

Melissa handed them each their fragrant old-fashioned pale orange rose-and-chrysanthemum bouquets before they headed to the chapel's vestibule. She took a seat in the front pew, holding Cassidy on her lap, while Effie's father waited with the boys to help give her away.

All traces of Remington's accident had been cleaned, and Colt stood alongside his brother's wheelchair. The pony plan had been ditched in favor of the boys stepping forward to give their mother away. But first, it was Mabel's turn.

The wedding planner ushered in the bridesmaids in their pumpkin-toned dresses. They all looked lovely with fall-themed bouquets filled with colorful mums and ivy.

The pews had been adorned with swags of mums and ivy and tulle, and on the altar sat a floral arch made of the same. There were also heart-shaped ivy topiaries and hundreds and hundreds of glowing candles.

A harpist began the wedding march and Effie stood back with the boys to watch her grandmother marry.

Marsh looked stoic, yet beyond handsome in his role as Wallace's best man.

Mabel insisted it would be bad luck for Effie to see Marsh before their ceremony, so she'd promoted a bridesmaid to the role of matron of honor.

Once Wallace and Mabel were pronounced husband and wife, they paraded down the aisle to make way for Effie.

As the harpist played the bridal march for the second time, Effie fought her hands' light tremble.

"Ready?" she asked her father and the boys.

"Only if you are," her dad said. "You look beautiful."

"Thank you, Dad." She hugged him, and the boys agreed that she looked *extra-especially* pretty. "Sorry you're having to give me away again."

"No worries. Marsh and I got to talk quite a bit this afternoon, and he seems like he's got a good head on his shoulders. If I were a betting man, I'd put money on this marriage being one that'll stick."

She laughed and cried.

"Stop that blubbering." He offered her a tissue. "Your mom said she'd have my hide if I said or did anything that ruined your makeup."

She laughed some more, and then her big moment finally arrived. The boys preceded her, with Colt pushing his brother's wheelchair. Her father strode behind them. She took her time with her walk, making sure she forever imprinted Marsh's handsome, stoic features in her mind.

Not until this very moment did she realize that for all of her tiptoeing around the issue of loving him, she did. She loved him with every bit of her heart—a good thing, she thought with a secret smile, considering she was on the verge of marrying the man.

She finally reached the altar, where the minister asked, "Who gives this woman's hand in marriage?"

"We do," her boys and father loudly said in practiced unison.

All present shared a good-natured chuckle.

Effie hugged her father one last time as a single woman, then took a deep breath before grasping the outstretched hands of Marsh, the man with whom she would happily spend the rest of her life.

MARSH COULDN'T BREATHE.

He tried focusing on Effie—how beautiful she looked in her dress, and the way her smile lit her eyes to the angelic blue green to which he'd first been drawn.

He tried…but failed.

All his brain allowed him to see was Remington, not in his wheelchair, but lying on the floor with blood pooling around him. So much blood. It was everywhere. What if he couldn't save him? What if just like Tucker, Remington died, too? How would Marsh ever explain that loss to Effie? He'd always considered himself to be a strong man, but if he'd been unable to bear losing his son, how would she cope with losing hers? Worse yet, Marsh would have been solely to blame. He'd bought the damned ponies in the first place. He should have known better. The twins were too young.

Thoughts raced faster and faster through his mind until he had to fight to keep himself from making a scene by covering his ears with his hands.

The ringing had grown so loud it hurt.

What was happening? He saw the minister's lips move, and then Effie's, but he couldn't hear their voices.

Finally, a voice broke through, but it was his own. "I-I'm sorry," he said to Effie. "I can't do this."

"What do you mean?" she asked, tone laced with concern. "Are you sick? What's wrong?"

Marsh couldn't vocalize what he could only feel—that he wasn't fit to become a father to her precious baby girl and sons. And so instead of talking, he ran.

Chapter Nineteen

"Mommy?" Colt asked, "Where's Mr. Marsh going? He promised not to leave. Doesn't he wanna to be our dad?"

"Of course, he does, sweetheart." Even though Colt's suspicion was exactly what Effie feared, she at least temporarily protected her son's fragile heart. "Marsh has a stomachache. I'm going to get him medicine, and then we'll be right back."

Colt's wide eyes said he wasn't so sure.

Remington was crying.

All of the guests started talking at once.

Wallace and Jacinda and Clive, Marsh's father, argued over who should chase after the groom.

"Everyone—" Effie said, while Marsh's family bickered back and forth "—if you'll please be patient, I'm going to grab the groom some antacid. He overdid it on last night's barbecue."

Nervous titters accompanied her out the door. Of course, no one believed her, but what her guests thought didn't matter. The only hearts that needed protecting belonged to her twin sons.

"Marsh?" she hollered upon reaching the parking lot.

She spotted him surging down a hiking trail.

Her ivory satin shoes were hardly suitable for the rocky terrain, but at the moment, nothing mattered more than successfully completing her wedding day—which meant she'd need an amenable groom.

"Marsh! Wait up!"

He only walked faster. "Go away! I'm no good for you—especially, not your kids."

"Pardon my French," she managed while running to catch up, "but that's horseshit! You're five times the man my ex ever was! The twins adore you, but right now you're walking a tightrope where they're concerned. They've already had their hearts shattered by their real dad. You promised them—and me—that you'd never leave, so what are you doing?"

He stopped.

"I covered for you back at the church, but my little white lie is only going to be good for so long."

He turned to her, and his tears came as a crushing blow. "I do love you, Effie. You and the boys and Cass. But when Remington fell, and all I could do was stand there in a fog, something inside me snapped. I realized I'm useless. You need someone whole. Even worse, I'm afraid of what might happen to me if I were to lose one or, God forbid, all of you."

"Key word—*might*. I'm living proof that life sure doesn't hand out guarantees—especially when it comes to relationships. If it helps, I feel just as vulnerable about my dependence on *you*. We've all grown to need you." She held him tight, praying she conveyed one iota of how much she'd grown to care. "Remember how Colt used to behave when you first came into our lives? He was smart-mouthed and sassy."

"Still is," he said.

"True." For the second time in an hour, Effie found herself laughing and crying. "But look how far he's come. He was uncontrollable, and now, with your help, he's starting to recognize when he's wrong. That's all because of you. What happened to Remington was an accident."

"So was what happened to Tucker, but he died. Who's to say I'm not bad luck?"

"Now, you're being stupid. You were a doll to buy the twins those ponies—and helmets. Who said they'd be fine not wearing them?"

He remained silent.

"That's right, me. Who insisted on riding ponies down the aisle of an already cramped chapel?"

He was silent again.

"That's right, Mabel and Wallace. If you want to play the blame game, I can point fingers all day, but here's the thing—none of them are directed toward you. I love you, Marsh. I don't know how or when it happened, but you've come to mean the world to me. If you no longer want to marry me, I guess I'll have to live with that fact, and I'll break it gently to the boys. But with every part of my being, I believe you do want to marry me and help me raise not just my children, but *ours*." She hugged him again. "And that's what they are, Marsh—yours and mine. Someday, God willing, we'll have more. But for now, please come back to the church with me, tell everyone you've got an upset stomach from barbecue, then let's get this wedding over with so we can get on with living the rest of our lives."

"I can't believe you'd even want to still marry me."

"Shocker—I do." On her tiptoes, she kissed him long and hard, until he was groaning and pressing her close enough that she recognized how much she was looking forward to their honeymoon.

He took her hand and kissed her still-empty ring finger. "With all the commotion over Remington, I forgot to buy you a fancy diamond engagement ring."

"Marsh Langtree, don't you know me well enough by now to realize I don't need a fancy ring? All I need is you."

He kissed her again, and then they walked hand in hand toward the chapel. Behind age-old paned windows, candles glowed, guiding them to their shared future.

Outside, Effie tightened her grip on his hand. "What you really went through—no one knows about but me. Forgive yourself. Grant yourself permission to love my boys the way they love you."

He nodded, kissing her again. "Thank you, Effie. Not just for saving my pride, but literally not just once, but now twice saving my life."

"Right back at you. Marry me?"

"I can't wait."

They walked into the chapel together, and, sandwiched between two smiling boys, said their vows.

They'd been through so much, yet from here on out, Effie knew they'd spend the rest of their lives together, happily ever after, secure in the knowledge that no matter what obstacles fate tossed in their shared paths, they'd tackle them as a team. United in spirit, souls and love.

Epilogue

On a sunny Saturday afternoon in May, Marsh sat in a crowd of hundreds, holding squirming Cassidy on his lap while Colt and Remington leaned in on both sides. Wallace and Mabel shared the row, as did his parents and Effie's. The Colorado Springs temperature was pleasantly warm for an outdoor graduation, and he couldn't be more impressed with his wife as she accepted her RN degree.

"I'm crazy proud of you," he said when he finally got to hold her again after the ceremony.

"Thank you." She kissed him before moving on to hug the rest of their family. "Thanks to all of you for sharing this with me. I never thought this day would come, but with Marsh's help…" She squealed. "I did it!"

Remington had long since healed, and he and Colt shared in her happy dance.

"Do you know where you're going to work?" Jacinda asked.

"For now—at least until the boys are older—I'm going to be the nurse at their school. I know it's not glamorous, but when their teacher told me the school's current nurse was retiring, I submitted my résumé to the principal and was hired."

"I love that you'll get to be with them," Melissa said. As usual, she'd once again cabbaged on to Cassidy and gave her a jiggle. She said to the baby, "I especially love that I get to spend my days with you." Effie's folks had sold their home in Oklahoma City and were in the process of building on a section of Mabel's land.

Officially, the land now belonged to Effie and Marsh, but to Effie, it would always be her grandmother's.

The group shared a steak lunch, then headed to Effie's official Maysville graduation party that was being hosted by Patricia.

When Effie finally stole a moment alone with her husband, she took his hand and led him to the pool's quiet side.

"Mmm…" Marsh said after thoroughly kissing her. "It's been nice visiting with family and friends, but is it wrong that I've been craving some quality alone time?" He'd officially retired from the Navy and now offered riding lessons to kids from town and the surrounding area. His schedule was so full that between her studies and his work ethic, they hardly shared time together.

"About that…"

He arched his head back and groaned. "Don't tell me—you've decided to jump right back into school for your master's?"

"Not exactly." She'd been debating how to tell him. She assumed he'd be happy, but what if he was more scared? She knew Tucker would always occupy a chunk of Marsh's heart. Did he have room for one more special person? Unsure how to broach the subject, she just blurted her news. "I'm pregnant."

"Wait—what?" He shook his head. "For real?"

She nodded. "I didn't want to say anything until I was sure. I had an ob-gyn friend test me, and it was positive. I'm about six weeks along. That's another reason I'd like to work at the boys' school. I'll have my summers free."

She worried when, for the longest time, he was quiet. "Marsh? Talk to me. What's wrong?"

"Not a thing." He shook his head, then smiled. In the shadows, she watched his gaze fill with unshed tears. "This was supposed to be your special day, so how come I got the best present?"

"You're happy?"

"Of course I'm happy. I'm thrilled. This is incredible. Tell me everything. So you're already six weeks along? Is it a boy or girl—never mind. As long as he or she is healthy, I don't care." He knelt to kiss her belly. "I already love you."

Effie's heart swelled.

Her husband's reaction couldn't have been more perfect. Just like their shared lives.

* * * * *

MILLS & BOON®

Cherish™

EXPERIENCE THE ULTIMATE RUSH OF FALLING IN LOVE

A sneak peek at next month's titles...

In stores from 2nd June 2016:

- **His Cinderella Heiress** – Marion Lennox *and* **Marriage, Maverick Style!** – Christine Rimmer
- **The Bridesmaid's Baby Bump** – Kandy Shepherd *and* **Third Time's the Bride!** – Merline Lovelace

In stores from 16th June 2016:

- **Bound by the Unborn Baby** – Bella Bucannon *and* **His Surprise Son** – Wendy Warren
- **Wedded for His Royal Duty** – Susan Meier *and* **The BFF Bride** – Allison Leigh

Available at WHSmith, Tesco, Asda, Eason, Amazon and Apple

Just can't wait?
Buy our books online a month before they hit the shops!
visit www.millsandboon.co.uk

These books are also available in eBook format!

Nikolai Drakos is determined to have his revenge against the man who destroyed his sister. So stealing his enemy's intended fiancé seems like the perfect solution! Until Nikolai discovers that woman is Ella Davies...

Read on for a tantalising excerpt from Lynne Graham's 100th book,

BOUGHT FOR THE GREEK'S REVENGE

'Mistress,' Nikolai slotted in cool as ice.

Shock had welded Ella's tongue to the roof of her mouth because he was sexually propositioning her and nothing could have prepared her for that. She wasn't drop-dead gorgeous... *he* was! Male heads didn't swivel when Ella walked down the street because she had neither the length of leg nor the curves usually deemed necessary to attract such attention. Why on earth could he be making *her* such an offer?

'But we don't even know each other,' she framed dazedly. 'You're a stranger...'

'If you live with me I won't be a stranger for long,' Nikolai pointed out with monumental calm. And the very sound of that inhuman calm and cool forced her to flip round and settle distraught eyes on his lean darkly handsome face.

'You can't be serious about this!'

'I assure you that I am deadly serious. Move in and I'll forget your family's debts.'

'But it's a *crazy* idea!' she gasped.

'It's not crazy to me,' Nikolai asserted. 'When I want anything, I go after it hard and fast.'

Her lashes dipped. Did he want her like that? Enough to track her down, buy up her father's debts, and try and buy rights to her and her body along with those debts? The very idea of that made her dizzy and plunged her brain into even greater turmoil. 'It's immoral... it's blackmail.'

'It's definitely *not* blackmail. I'm giving you the benefit of a choice you didn't have before I came through that door,' Nikolai Drakos fielded with a glittering cool. 'That choice is yours to make.'

'Like hell it is!' Ella fired back. 'It's a complete cheat of a supposed offer!'

Nikolai sent her a gleaming sideways glance. 'No the real cheat was you kissing me the way you did last year and then saying no and acting as if I had grossly insulted you,' he murmured with lethal quietness.

'You *did* insult me!' Ella flung back, her cheeks hot as fire while she wondered if her refusal that night had started off his whole chain reaction. What else could possibly be driving him?

Nikolai straightened lazily as he opened the door. 'If you take offence that easily, maybe it's just as well that the answer is no.'

MILLS & BOON®

Mills & Boon have been at the heart of romance since 1908... and while the fashions may have changed, one thing remains the same: from pulse-pounding passion to the gentlest caress, we're always known how to bring romance alive.

Now, we're delighted to present you with these irresistible illustrations, inspired by the vintage glamour of our covers. So indulge your wildest dreams and unleash your imagination as we present the most iconic Mills & Boon moments of the last century.

Visit **www.millsandboon.co.uk/ArtofRomance** to order yours!